Cover by Jim Wilmink

ISBN: 978-1-943180-45-5

ISBN: 978-1-943180-47-9 paperback

Moonlight Magnolia Press, Lexington, KY 40515

This is a work of fiction. Names, characters, places and incidents either are the product of the author's imagination or are used fictitiously, and any resemblance to actual persons, living or dead, business establishments, events, or locales is entirely coincidental.

For everyone who didn't want Jane to retire.

JANE DOE 4 | CHARLOTTE

THE JANE DOE BOOKS

KRIS CALVERT

ALSO BY KRIS CALVERT

Sex, Lies & Sweet Tea – Book One

Sex, Lies & Lipstick – Book Two

Sex, Lies & Pearls – Book Three

Sex, Lies & Lace – Book Four

Sex, Lies & Bourbon - Book Five

Sex, Lies & Black Tie - Book Six

Sex, Lies & Diamonds - Book Seven

Sex, Lies & Champagne - Book Eight

Sex, Lies & Leather - Book Nine

Sex, Lies & Rock n Roll - Book Ten

Fate, Snow & Mistletoe - A Sex and Lies Holiday Novella

Jane Doe 1 Scarlett

Jane Doe 2 Alice

Jane Doe 3 Catherine

Jane Doe 4 Charlotte

Beauty

Lead Me From Temptation

Deliver Me From Evil

Be Mine – a Valentine's Day Novella

Sparks Fly – an Independence Day Novella

Roses are Wrong, Violets Taboo

Witchin' in the Kitchen - A Halloween Novella

Coming
The Fox Tales Series
Sex, Lies & Tequila

JANE DOE
CHARLOTTE
4

BY KRIS CALVERT

"Charlotte put her victim to sleep before eating it."

— E.B. WHITE, CHARLOTTE'S WEB

DAY TWO THOUSAND FIVE HUNDRED AND FIFTY-FIVE | 2000 HOURS

She blew at the stray hair stuck to her lip with a puff of exasperation and eyed the keys she'd dropped on the ground. The front door to the turn-of-the-century building gleamed with fresh black paint, the pungent fumes of which hung in the air like a fog as the painter stood back to admire his work. She took short breaths to keep from inhaling the stench, finally resorting to holding her breath. Stepping just inside the door, her stomach rumbled with a gurgled sigh. She'd been in the library nonstop for the past eighteen hours, which meant two things: she was hungry, and her PhD thesis was done. Tomorrow, she would defend it.

"God kväll, miss," the doorman said with a welcoming smile. "Or should I say, Doktor?"

He'd asked the same question for the past week, and each time she gave the same answer. "Inte än." Not yet.

She brushed past him to get her mail, not engaging in further conversation. He knew better; she wasn't much of a talker. She never had been. Taking the three flights of stairs to the top floor, she unlocked the door to the six-bedroom, three-bath apartment on the corner of Sibyllegatan and Östermalmsgatan she'd called home for the past six years, in Stockholm, Sweden.

Exhausted from the long hours—her body was drained, her brain, wired—she locked the door behind her and tossed her keys and leather messenger bag on top of the dining room table before scanning the expanse of her home. Finally sinking into the couch, she relaxed her neck to stare at the ceiling above her.

Just one day away from finishing her PhD at the Kungliga Tekniska högskolan Royal Institute of Technology—better known as KTH—she felt an emptiness she'd not known for years. It was a cross between relief and the unknown of what comes next. Her time in Stockholm had been important and profound. Free from everything she'd left behind in the States, she'd connected with interesting and like-minded people, gained knowledge beyond her wildest expectations, and honed her Krav Maga skills—all while stretching her biggest muscle to date—her mind.

Casting her gaze around the room, she surveyed the many trinkets she'd accumulated over the past few years. None of them were of real value, mostly knickknacks she'd picked up around town while shopping the streets. When she arrived, all she had were the clothes on her back and the contents of her backpack: one letter, one file, a small metal box, and a photo of her mother. Everything else in the home with original parquet floors and kakelugn ceramic fireplaces, she'd added in the past two thousand or so days.

The apartment was, of course, too big for one person, and the few colleagues she allowed into her life and home always asked why she didn't rent the one room with its own entrance and staircase to a back alley. She would simply shrug and say, "I like the quiet of living alone." She never told them she required more than one escape route from her own home.

She'd settled into her new life with remarkable ease—at least when she first arrived. Accustomed to high octane, do-or-die conditions, she was ready and willing to quiet her active mind. At first it did her good to set herself apart from all that she'd been through, but after a few months, she was bored, and her past life began to catch up with her—at least in her head. The nightmares were frequent; the second-guessing of her own actions and outcomes on repeat. Worst of all was the longing—a longing for something she could never have.

Her plan after spending a year in New York City had always been to fade into obscurity and focus on her education. She raced through her undergraduate and master's degrees in only four years, leaving her with only one option: to continue her studies and earn a PhD. Tomorrow would mark her finest moment of the past two years—defending her thesis. What came after was much like the background of her existence to the few friends she had in Stockholm—murky.

Off the couch and into her bedroom, she opened the closet. The meticulously arranged items in mostly earth tones a testament to her minimalist mindset. She essentially wore the same outfit each day in a different color, mixing and matching as the week went on. It wasn't that she couldn't afford to buy finer clothes, she had more money than she knew how to spend; what she lacked was the desire to spend it on anything other than school and food. Besides, Stockholm was the perfect location to wear somewhat utilitarian clothing, and she was all for function above fashion. Still, like her wardrobe, what she'd envisioned as a life filled with endless possibilities, in reality had become the same day over and over again.

She changed into sweatpants and a long-sleeved shirt, pulling her brown hair from her face to pile it atop her head. Back in the main room, she slipped a heavy cardigan over her shoulders before opening the doors to the balcony. As she leaned into the ancient concrete railing, the crisp Swedish air rushed across her skin and she took a full and cleansing breath, recalling all the hours she'd spent studying, researching, innovating and writing. It had been a long road, but school had given her a sense of purpose. Now, she was at a loss on how to proceed with her life.

She didn't want to teach—too many eyes. She didn't want to work in research at KTH—too boring.

"What *do* you want?" She asked the question, sending it into the universe on a gust of frigid wind.

A knock rang out at her front door, and before she could ask, he called out to her. "I know you're in there. Open up."

She answered the door, hanging onto the frame to stare him in the face. "*How* did you know I was here?"

"The biblioteksassistent told me you'd left for the night," he said, stroking his blond beard with one hand while holding a grease-stained paper bag in the other.

Wolfgang Larrson was, for lack of a better term, a

fuck buddy. A brilliant physicist with a decently sculpted body, he'd kept her warm on the nights when she agreed to his company. He was her plus-one to the university functions that were mandatory, and he was a nice enough guy, but Wolf wanted more from their relationship. She didn't do *more*. She was focused on her plan. It was all she'd concentrated on for the past six years.

Besides, she'd tried her hand at what she thought was love. Turns out, it wasn't so lovely after all.

"Wolf," she said, with slight contempt. "I'm too tired to deal with this tonight."

"*This*?" he asked.

She closed the door behind him, once again noticing the bag in his hand, as well as the brown paper package peeking out of his coat pocket. Still hyper-observant, she constantly watched everyone in her presence. "You know what I mean."

"I'm not here to add to your stress, I know tomorrow's your big day. I simply thought you might be hungry. For reasons I will never understand, you forget to eat, so I stopped by Josef's Grill."

She dismissed his comment, focusing her eyes on the bag and the notion of what might be inside. It wasn't that she hadn't adapted to the food in her new homeland, but there *were* things she missed about America—one of them being corndogs. She stared down Wolf Larrson and watched him raise the bag high in the air. He was tall. Tall enough to hold her dinner above his head where she couldn't reach—dangling the proverbial carrot.

"Before I give you anything," Wolf said, lowering the bag, but not relinquishing. "I want an apology."

She bristled at his demand and took a step away.

"Jävla." Wolf cursed under his breath and handed over the bag, before pulling a red bandana from his pocket to wipe the grease from his hand.

"Thank you," she said, peeking inside. "But I don't want company tonight. I have less than twelve hours before I defend my thesis and present my project."

"I know," he said, still wrestling the bandana. "I only want to wash the corndog grease from my hands and I'll be gone."

Wolf walked toward the kitchen while speaking over his shoulder. "Did you see the news from America."

"What news?" she asked, sticking her nose into the bag for a whiff of the warm dogs.

"The bombing."

The hair on the back of her neck stood at attention, and she struggled to maintain her usual stoic poise. "Bombing?"

"The New York City subway," he said, turning on the water. "Three suicide bombers. It looked horrific. It happened this morning somewhere in Manhattan— I believe it was beneath Times Square during rush hour. The blast killed a member of the American Parliament—the Senate."

She looked at the clock on the wall. Five hours ahead of New York, it was only two in the afternoon in the States. She turned on the television, quickly finding BBC International. The story was front and center. Senator Maggie Thompson was on the train platform when the bombs were detonated. The carnage was horrific. As the announcer spoke of casualty numbers, Jane closed her eyes to calm the silent fury rising from deep within her. "That sack of assholes finally did it," she said under her breath.

"What?" Wolf asked, quickly coming to her side. Together they watched the wounded limp out of the train station exits covered in soot and blood.

"Tragic," she muttered, unable to tear her eyes from the bloodbath.

"Absolutely tragic. Do you have friends in New York City?"

The memory of him flashed through her mind. Her fingers deep in his hair—his strong hands all over her body. "No."

She turned off the television, and her back on the gruesome scenes.

"Hey," Wolf said, rubbing her shoulders with genuine sincerity. "What might I do to help you? I've brought you food, but I'm available for any type of stress relief you might need," he said, brushing a stray hair from her neck to plant a lingering kiss below her ear.

When her body didn't respond and she didn't answer, Wolf took a full breath and stepped away. "I'm off then," he said, his ruddy face a canvas of disappointment.

Without a word, she walked him to the door, her mind no longer focused on her thesis and presentation, but Midtown Manhattan. "Thank you, Wolf. For the…" She hesitated, searching for her words. "For dinner."

He nodded and turned to leave without saying goodbye. She looked away as she shut the door, her mind focused on New York City. When Wolf stopped it from closing with his foot, she bristled with irritation. "What?"

Wolf took the small package from the pocket of his coat. "I almost forgot," he said, "The doorman asked me to bring it up. I guess someone left it for you."

She arched her brow, offering him an upturned palm.

"Something from an admirer? Perhaps a token from Dr. Lundgren? Does he too know you don't care for flowers?"

The rough brown paper grazed her skin, and a familiar feeling washed over her. She found herself catching her breath. "It's not from Dr. Lundgren," she said, closing the door in his face.

"Good luck tomorrow!" Wolf shouted from the other side.

She tossed the package on the coffee table in front of the couch. On autopilot, she closed the balcony doors and drew the curtains. Walking to the kitchen for a glass of water, she felt her throat tighten. It was the kind of tension she'd buried long ago. Still, she shook it off.

The kitchen was very much like the rest of the turn-of-the-century apartment, well preserved yet void of much personality. Her home was nicer than most in Stockholm, yet despite its comforts and the six years she'd spent within its walls, it lacked warmth and a feeling of home.

After a year or so, she realized that she had no beautiful moments to recall when it came to comprehending a stable and loving home—no happy childhood memories. When she did allow her feelings to creep in, the profound void she felt inside rendered her ill-equipped to fill any space she occupied with a sense of comfort. The home was undeniably beautiful, but other than a stolen photo, the space she occupied felt very much like the inside of her mind. Perfectly suitable but lacking a soul.

From the cabinet she pulled a single glass from the set of eight on the bottom shelf. There wasn't much food in the pantry either, only the essentials. And just like her bed, the refrigerator was cold and empty. There was, however, a place for everything and everything was in its place, making her apartment feel more like a military barracks than the million-dollar property it was.

Walking to the couch, she grabbed a cloth napkin from a drawer on her way out of the kitchen and sat, eager to take the first bite of her dinner.

Wolf had bought her not one, but two corndogs. This time his desire to give her more was completely appreciated. Two bites in, she stared at the brown paper package. She had asked for an older book from the stacks during the last stages of writing her thesis, but that time had long come and gone.

With a heavy sigh filled with anger and regret, she turned the television on once again, increasing the volume just in time to hear the fatality score in New York City: "...twelve dead, and dozens injured. Among the victims killed was Senator Maggie Thompson, head of the Armed Services Committee and ranking member of the Appropriations Committee. Senator Thompson, of course, had quite a presidential campaign run, before nodding out to New Hampshire Governor Wilbur Franklin. She was the presumed favorite to be Governor Franklin's vice-presidential pick. Maggie Thompson was also a wife and a mother of three young children."

As she watched the video of Midtown Manhattan

unfold, she found herself thinking of him—his strong embrace, his deep laugh, his warm blue eyes that crinkled when he smiled. Was he there? Was he safe?

Casting off a past that could easily ensnare her, she stuck the corndog in her mouth, clearing her throat and her mind, before unwrapping the parcel.

A red hardback, the spine was old, and the gold stamping worn. She couldn't quite make out the title in the low light of the table lamp beside her, so she opened it to the first page.

With a gasp, she immediately tossed it back onto the coffee table with a thud.

Dropping the corndog into the greasy bag, she rubbed her temples and stared at the book. One thought filled her mind and escaped her lips. "No."

The cover board poked out through the frayed red linen at the book's corner, while a million scenarios raced through her mind. Immediately on high alert, she was off the couch, ripping apart the duct tape that secured the forty-five caliber Glock under the dining room table.

Before she could react, he was on her.

A garrote sliced through the air, tightening mercilessly around her neck. The masked man in black yanked with savage force, the cold wire biting deep into her skin. With every ounce of strength, she pushed her body backward, using her weight to prevent him from arching her spine. If he got the upper hand, it was over.

Her fingers clawed behind her neck, desperately seeking the wire. She found it and clung to it with all her might. Keeping the pressure away from her closing throat, she opened her airway just enough to stave off unconsciousness. Her vision blurred at the edges, but she twisted into his body, driving her fist into his groin.

The first blow landed with a sickening thud, but it wasn't enough. She struck again, the second a more violent blow. His grip faltered, and the garrote loosened just enough for her to catch one precious breath of air.

Seizing the moment, she punched her fist into his neck, her knuckles cracking against his Adam's apple with a sickening crunch. He staggered back with a gasp, his balance faltering as he bent over in pain.

But she wasn't done.

Ever relentless, she drove her knee up and into his chin once—and then again with even greater power, forcing his head backwards with a brutal snap.

He winced in pain and while her assailant was stunned, she seized the opportunity to wrap her arm around his neck, locking him in a deadly chokehold. He thrashed, fists hammering at her arms, but the fight was leaving him. She could feel his strength ebb away with every second, his blows weaker and more desperate, until the breath left his body.

With a final, brutal twist, she wrenched his head up and back. She not only heard it but felt the snap of his neck in her hands.

His body collapsed on the ground in a heap of defeat.

Without missing a beat, she picked up the gun she'd dropped, clearing each room with military precision. Only when convinced she was alone did she take a full breath.

Now on autopilot, she walked with purpose to the laundry room, moving the dryer with a grunt. Two shoves later, she was on her knees, her fingers prying at the floorboards. A faint creak of wood echoed inside the silent room, and she glanced over her shoulder, calming her breath and thumping heart.

She lifted the loosened board, exposing the hidden compartment below. Inside was her coyote brown backpack containing cash, passport, two more guns with ammo, three knives including a switchblade, zip-ties, duct tape, a prepaid burner phone, and a change of clothes including a black zip-up hoodie.

Bringing the bag to the surface, she sat back on her heels, wiping the sweat from her brow with a ragged breath. It was time to go.

Adapt. Improvise. Overcome.

She walked through her house, picking up the two battery packs charging on the kitchen countertop before dropping the go-bag by the door. Then she paced the room back and forth only twice. It was time to face it. She'd been found.

She sat, opening the book once more, staring at the title page. Charlotte's Web, by E.B. White. Her shoulders dropped and she whispered into the worn pages, fanning them through the thumb of one hand while gripping the gun in the other. *"Cocksuckingmotherfuckingsonofabitch."*

Outside, a car backfired and she cocked the gun in a fluid motion, ready to fire. She exhaled, then nodded to herself, allowing her adrenaline and rote skills to kick in. Taking the photo of her mother from the bookshelf, she tossed it in her bag before unlocking the top drawer of her desk nearby. Inside was the police report of her humble beginnings, along with the metal box filled with everything she truly held dear.

Scanning the room for anything important, she

pulled the SIM card from her personal phone and flushed it down the toilet.

When she unmasked her would-be killer, his was a face she didn't recognize. She grabbed his ankles and dragged him through her home to the back door to the waste chute used by the people in her building. Without ceremony or thought, she tossed his lifeless body into the waste-to-energy incinerator. One thing she loved about the Swedes was that only one percent of their trash went a landfill. The rest was incinerated and used for heat. With any luck, he would be burned beyond recognition when or even *if* his body was ever found.

She gave the apartment one last look, turned off the TV, and tossed the book into her backpack before slinging it over her shoulder. Gripping her leather satchel and the paper bag with the remaining corn-dog, she closed the door to the only stable home she'd ever known and walked away.

Without taking a beat, she spilled out onto the streets of Stockholm, head down, gun in her pocket. She'd spent the last seven years moving forward, yet it seemed she was destined to return to the life she once knew. But she didn't look back. Jane never looked back.

After checking into a dive motel in the Husby area of the city, Jane sat on the worn bedcovers with a loaded gun in her lap and another by her side. She'd waited all night for the sun to rise. In three hours' time, she was to present her research and conclusions, as well as her project to her advisor and other academic experts in the field of bioengineering. But Jane's mind was far from the hard work of the past few years. Her attention remained solely on what was staring her in the face: a copy of *Charlotte's Web* and the life she'd left behind.

Running her hands across the worn linen hardback, she opened it to the inside back flap. There she found the all-too-familiar library card filled with the numbers she would need to decode the Ottendorf Cipher contained within. The question was, did she want to?

They would never stop looking for her. It was what happened to people like Jane, agents who knew too much and had seen even more. Jane knew that place where those in power mingled and made plans.

She not only thrived in that environment; she'd survived and walked away.

When she joined the Coywolf Project, she was naïve, imprudent, and filled with anger. She knew all of the targets and their numbers and had done extensive research on every single one. But there was one man—she had every piece of intel on him memorized like her life depended on it. He became an obsession, and she watched him like a hawk even though he wasn't her charge. Back then, Jane had only one thing on her mind: kill Siad al Daleel ul Khyayraat—Number Three on *The List*. She'd taken out many on the United States government's list of known terrorists, but as much as she'd hoped and prayed for the day to end his life, Three's number was never assigned to her.

As it turned out, Siad knew just as much about her as she did about him. But the revelation that he was Jane's biological father was something her mind and heart struggled to comprehend. It was far beyond the boundaries of what she could intellectually or emotionally process.

Jane ended his life, and eventually, after hiding out and falling in and out of love, she left the United States for what she believed would be for good.

Jane made her getaway with a bit of help from the few she trusted, but in the back of her mind, she always knew *they* would come for her. She just didn't think they would come so soon.

At present, Jane had two choices: she could cut and run, or she could defend her thesis, explain the significance of her research, present and demonstrate her project, and walk away as Dr. Jane Ellison. Her plan was always to use the alias Jennifer Dashwood, but after learning her mother's name, she thought it was only fitting to leave Doe behind. She never dreamed she would need to become that person again.

Taking the burner phone from her backpack, she powered it up with a battery before plugging in a clean SIM card. Then, using an international calling card she'd purchased with cash, she called a number she'd memorized from her past. It was the middle of the night in Virginia, but he answered on the first ring.

"Hudson."

His voice was just as she remembered; soft but filled with the confident timbre of a man who'd weathered many storms. "Peter?"

"Jane?" Surprise laced his breathy reply.

Jane mirrored his shock, astounded he'd recognized her voice. "Yes," she said, almost giddy that he knew her right away.

He was direct and to the point. "Tell me what you need."

One of the many traits Jane admired about Dr. Peter Hudson, the CEO and head of the billion-dollar defense contractor Maxtronix, was that he knew she wouldn't call unless she was in trouble. He, like her, cut right to the core.

"I've been...*found.*"

"What's your extraction point?" he asked, his tone clipped and strictly business.

Jane looked at herself in the hotel's faded mirror before glancing at the digital clock by the bedside. If she showered and left in the next thirty minutes, she could just make her designated appointment at KTH.

Jane hesitated. "I have something I need to do. Something I *want* to do."

"I'm asking again: what's your extraction point?"

"Tonight," Jane said with confidence. "Oslo."

"Tonight?"

"Yes," she said, convincing herself and straightening her posture. "If I'm not at the train station by midnight, don't wait. You'll know I didn't make it out."

"You'll make it," Peter said with confidence.

Jane hung up without a goodbye. Then digging into the bottom of her bag, she pulled out the change of clothes she'd packed long ago. Black pants and a blue sweater, it wasn't the fancy suit she'd bought for her big day, but it would have to do.

She showered in record time, pulled her hair into a bun, and got dressed, noticing the ligature marks and bruising around her neck—courtesy of her would-be assassin. "Are you burning in hell yet, you shitbag? Or just the incinerator," she muttered thinking of the man she'd killed while straightening her sweater and smoothing back her hair.

Still, she had bigger problems than a dead assassin. She couldn't bring her bags into KTH; the guns and knives would set off the metal detectors. Jane needed to leave immediately to give herself enough time to stop by her campus office.

Jane repacked the bags, knowing at some point in the next twenty-four hours, she may be forced to part with one or both in order to run for her life. Then, while shifting the packs of money and ammo in the bottom of her backpack, she saw it—the scarf belonging to Matt Matthews. The handsome journalist had worn it the day Jane met him in Atlanta—the day he'd flirted with her, all windburned and full of charm. She'd taken it from a pile of his clothes after a long night of exquisite sex—or maybe it was making love.

Jane had spent countless hours over the past seven years reflecting on what happened. Yet despite all the time that had passed, she still couldn't untangle the knot of emotions that tightened inside her whenever her mind turned to Matt.

Dipping her nose into the scarf, she inhaled, hoping to find a glimpse of him. There was nothing.

She wrapped the scarf around her neck to cover the bruises and gave herself a fleeting glance before hauling a bag over each shoulder and leaving the motel.

As she took the Tunnelbana from the Husby station onto campus, the last thing on her mind was explaining *The Effect of Nanotechnology-enabled Smart Textiles to Monitor Soldier Health and Performance in Combat Environments*. But that was exactly how she planned to spend her last few moments in Stockholm. After, she would leave it all behind.

———

THE PRAISE FROM HER PROFESSORS, advisors and industry leaders was remarkable. Once she began the presentation, she operated with the efficiency and precision of a well-oiled machine. Explaining the technology and the impact it could have on the future of combat soldiers, the patch known as VitalWatch could not only monitor vital signs such as blood pressure and heart rate, to name a few, but it was also a GPS-enabled micro-camera and recording transmitter that captured video. Waterproof and resistant to debris, it would work for thirty to forty-five days before a new patch would need to replace it.

It was a peek into the world of the modern-day soldier and could be a crucial piece of combat gear, especially for those in high-threat areas and targets for capture. The best part was that it was virtually invisible to the naked eye.

It was evident to everyone in the room the excitement and passion Jane had for her ground-breaking invention. As she took the last question, Jane glanced at the clock just above the heads of the panel who'd grilled her for the past hour, hoping and praying she could grab the backpack from her office and catch a cab to the train station. If Jane hurried, and they didn't ask more questions, she could just make it.

"Jane," her advisor said, coming to his feet. "Congratulations!"

The room erupted in applause, and she couldn't help but smile. Jane knew she deserved this, but like so many of the pivotal moments in her life, she was on the run. When she declined their champagne toast, citing that she wasn't feeling her best and needed to leave, she wasn't lying. She *was* sick—sick from being back in the game.

Jane offered her thanks to everyone, then shocked her advisor, Dr. Lundgren, by throwing her arms around him for a tight embrace. "Thank you," she whispered into his shoulder. "For everything."

"Grattis. Congratulations," he said, pulling away and beaming with pride.

With a nod and a wave to the rest of the advisors and panel, Jane slung her leather satchel over her shoulder. She walked away, stopping only to take the silicon sheet containing the remaining VitalWatch patches from the presentation materials.

Out of the building and across campus, she made it to her office, skipping the elevator for the stairs. Jane knew there were cameras in every corner of the university, but it wasn't until that moment she felt as if she was being watched.

Deep voices echoed through the stairwell, and she ducked into a doorway, listening to the conversation. Jane was fluent in Swedish, and she knew right away they weren't looking for her. It was at that moment she realized: PhD or no PhD, she was Jane Doe once again.

Finally on her floor, she opened the door to her office and found not only her bag behind her desk, but a beaming Wolfgang Larrson.

"Grattis!" he shouted, slowly coming to his feet with resounding applause.

Jane's shoulders fell. Wolf was a fine man, but he always seemed to be in the wrong place at the wrong time—that was no more evident than today.

"Wolf," she sighed.

He held his arms wide, beckoning for a hug. "What? I thought you'd be excited."

Jane dropped the leather satchel on her shoulder into the chair by her desk, hanging her hands on her waist with a perturbed sigh.

"Wait," he said, confusion now painting his oblivious countenance. "What happened to the fancy suit you bought for today?"

"*Wolf.*"

"What's wrong? Oh no," he said with a gasp, before pulling her to his chest in a contested hug. "Did you not successfully defend?"

The question made Jane even more irate. The clock was ticking, and every second lost in Wolfgang Larrson's embrace was precious time she didn't have. "Of course I successfully defended my thesis, but that's not the point. You had no right to ambush me this way. You know I don't like surprises."

The old Jane would've put him to sleep, leaving him for the cleaning crew to discover. New Jane didn't have the luxury of drugs in her bag, nor did she want to give him a chop to the carotid artery to knock him out—even though that thought had crossed her mind. Jane would need to improvise. Pushing him away, she placed her hands on her hips, hoping he would catch her not-so-subtle hint to leave.

"Wow," he said, gathering his coat, his eyes cast to the floor.

Jane placed a hand on his shoulder in a feeble attempt to console him. "Look, Wolf, I'm taking a trip for a few weeks."

"What? Where are you going?"

"I don't know," she said. "The past couple of years have been grueling, and I think I deserve some time away."

Wolf stared at her, and Jane was, for the first time in a long time, questioning her ability to lie. "Are you coming back?" he asked.

Jane thought it an odd question considering her current circumstances, but at the same time, she knew there was no coming back from where she was going. She allowed one final lie to slip across her lips. "Of course, I'll be back. Here," she said, handing him a single key to her apartment. "Water my plants."

"Your plants?" he asked. "You only had the one I gave you, and I'm pretty sure you killed it."

"Yeah," Jane said, cupping his bearded face in her hand. "Unfortunately, I kill a lot of things."

Wolf eyed the key in his palm, then leaned in and kissed her. Jane allowed it. It seemed the perfect goodbye to a perfectly decent man. "Go," he said. "Do whatever it is you feel you need to do. I'll get your mail and keep an eye on the place."

Jane nodded, patting him on the chest with her open hand. "Thank you, Wolfie. You've been a good friend these past few years."

He pulled away, holding her at arm's length. "Friend? Do you sleep with all your friends?"

Jane kissed Wolfgang Larrson one more time before collecting the second bag from behind her desk. She opened the door and turned, smiling at him. "Only the ones I like."

THE CAB RIDE to the train station seemed to take an eternity, but Jane knew it was because she was anxious and everything seemed out of her control. It was at that moment she realized that while settling into her new life, perhaps she'd become a bit soft. It would take time for her to find her way back. Back to what, exactly, she had no idea.

When Jane finally arrived at the train station, she rushed to the ticket counter, then sprinted toward the platform. She made it just in time, catching the trail as the porter was closing the door. It would be another five hours before she would meet...*someone.* She didn't know who, only that she would know them when she saw them.

Finally settled into her seat, Jane pulled the book

from her bag and began not to decipher, but to read. *Charlotte's Web* was one of her favorite books growing up. Now, it would forever be just another tome in a long line of assignments.

After reading the first two chapters, Jane found the gumption to take the worn, hand-stamped library card from the back of the book. The series of numbers, which looked like due dates, were the page numbers, lines on that page, and numbered word in the line of text. She deciphered the location and the first two words and knew it meant only one thing: she was heading to Langley, Virginia.

OPERATION THUNDERSTRUCK.

DAY ONE | 1700 HOURS

Jane fought sleep. Between fending off death, readying herself to defend her thesis, and packing up on a moment's notice, she hadn't shut her eyes. She was running on pure adrenaline. Jane told herself she would sleep when she was safely departing Oslo for the United States.

By the time the train pulled into Sentralstasjon, better known as Oslo S, Jane was already on her feet. For the past six years, she'd lived with a pencil tucked behind her ear. Now, she had a gun tucked in the backside of her pants and a knife concealed in her boot.

The air was chilly as Jane stepped onto the platform. She'd failed to grab a winter coat when leaving the apartment and was now facing the consequences. With her hoodie pulled over her head, she scanned the train platform, looking for someone who might be there for her.

Jane hung back, pulling the burner phone from her back pocket and searching for a text of any sort. When there was nothing, she calmly put her phone away, instead looking for anything that seemed out of place. Jane casually looked left and right along the platform as passengers greeted each other with hugs and kisses.

Improvise. Adapt. Overcome.

Then, off the train four cars down, an elderly woman emerged. Likely in her nineties, she clutched a cane in one hand and carried a pocketbook that looked to be out of the closet of Queen Elizabeth II. Around her neck hung a hand-knitted red scarf with small pom poms on each end. Jane noticed but tried to avoid staring as she lingered, waiting for every passenger to disperse, hoping someone would stay behind on the train platform.

One by one, everyone disappeared until only Jane and the old woman in the red scarf remained.

The elderly lady regarded Jane. "Be a dear," she said, her British accent laced with the hoarse undertones of age. "Help me with my bag, would you?"

Jane was leery of anyone or anything that didn't fit her narrative of what *should* transpire upon her arrival in Oslo. Still, she leaned in to pick up the bag the porter had placed at the old woman's feet, noticing her orthopedic shoes and support hose. The swollen ankles told Jane this was, indeed, simply a little old lady in need of assistance. "Happy to. Which way are you going?"

She pointed toward the lobby of the train station, where Jane could only assume a loved one was waiting for her. The woman walked at a glacial pace, and Jane took the opportunity to scan the area for suspicious characters or her contact. The small white-haired woman had a hunchback and couldn't or wouldn't look up at Jane as they approached the main door.

Just inside, two men in black suits sat on opposite sides of the lobby. To Jane, they looked out of place, and that meant only one thing: they were there for her.

At the very moment Jane's heart rate began to rise, the elderly woman dropped her cane. Jane bent down to pick it up just as one of the men passed their way. Keeping her face to the floor and her hood over her head, Jane could hear the older woman say in a Norwegian Bokmål dialect, "Barnebarnet mitt er så hjelpsom." *My granddaughter is so helpful.*

Not raising her head, Jane lingered, pretending to adjust the sock inside her boot. When the black dress shoes were no longer in Jane's sight, she stood, offering the woman in the red scarf her cane and a timid smile. The little old lady looked up for the first time since asking for Jane's help, giving her a single reassuring nod.

Keeping a slow pace, Jane helped her through the main lobby door and street side. A black Tesla 3 pulled to the curb. "Our ride is here, dear," the woman said.

Jane opened the back door, helping the old woman to fold her arthritic body inside the car. "You sit up front," she said in a quiet but commanding tone.

Finally moving quickly, Jane closed the back door, opening the front passenger side, only to find there wasn't a driver. Glancing over her shoulder, Jane could see the men in black milling about the lobby and quickly climbed aboard.

When the door was securely closed, Jane fought the urge to turn and look the elderly woman in the face. "Who are you?" she asked, staring out into the midnight sky.

"Surely, you didn't believe you were the first of your kind."

Jane fidgeted in the front seat. "My *kind*?"

"I'm a Special Operations Executive. Retired," she said. "F Section. Code name Odile."

"F Section?" Jane asked. She'd heard about the women who acted as spies during World War Two, but in a million years, she never thought she would meet one.

"I was a courier and wireless operator for the Allied Forces in occupied France. I sent and received Morse code messages about planned sabotage operations," she said. "Risky business, that. And I was barely sixteen years old."

Before Jane could utter another word, the car pulled away from the curb, driving on its own. "Who's behind the wheel?" Jane asked, glancing at her in the rearview mirror.

The woman in the red scarf shrugged her shoulders. "I reckon it doesn't matter at this point in the game."

"I'm sorry," Jane began. "Who and how did—"

"No names, love. I'm supposed to get you to the airport. That's all I know, and there's no point in asking more. If the Gestapo couldn't get me to talk, neither will you."

Jane noticed the navigation system with a preset destination of Oslo Lufthave in Gardermoen. She settled in and took a deep breath. Even though dozens of questions about *Odile* buzzed through her head, Jane was merely a passenger for the next thirty miles.

When they arrived at the airport, the Tesla drove onto the private tarmac of the airfield and to a waiting jet. "Maxtronix must still be doing okay," Jane said under her breath. When the car came to a halt, she turned. "Thank you, Odile. Thank you for getting me...*out.*"

"We girls have to stick together. Best of luck to you, dear," she said with a single nod.

Jane picked up her bags, crisscrossing the straps over her shoulders. Jane stepped aboard the Gulfstream G650, noting that the jet was spacious enough to accommodate over a dozen passengers. Yet, aside from the flight crew and a single attendant, she was the only one on board.

"Good evening, ma'am," the flight attendant said before handing Jane a note. "May I get you anything? A drink?"

"Water." Jane waited until she was alone before opening the envelope.

Glad you made it to Oslo safely. Get some sleep. I'll see you in fourteen hours.

As the plane took off, the flight attendant was back with Jane's water and a dinner menu. "Heading home?" she asked.

"I'll have the steak and potatoes," Jane said, handing back the menu. "And...I don't really have a home."

Jane didn't know why she'd said it. She'd never made reference to where she lived, even while in Sweden for the past six years. Yet, somehow, leaving it all behind gave her the license or perhaps the courage to speak her truth into existence.

The attendant smiled. "You carry your roots with you and decide where they grow."

Jane appreciated the comment, but the closest she'd ever come to having a *home* was in Stockholm, and she'd more than uprooted. She'd cut down the tree.

DAY THREE | 1100 HOURS

J ane opened her eyes only when the flight attendant nudged her on the shoulder. "Sorry to wake you, but I need you to buckle up, miss. The captain is ready to land."

"Land?" Jane asked, rubbing her eyes. "Land where?"

The flight attendant smiled, clearly believing Jane was bewildered from her long sleep. "Washington, D.C., of course."

Jane nodded and straightened her body to sit upright on the long couch she'd used as a bed. She buckled up, then lifted the shade on the closest window. The sun was shining over the capital, and Jane wondered what was next. She knew Peter couldn't hide her away forever; whatever or whoever wanted her gone would eventually find her. But she'd made a decision: she wasn't running anymore.

Jane had seen the world and didn't want for anything. She had enough money to last her ten lifetimes, and she had loved and lost. And maybe, if the Buddhists were right and samsara was real, she would have the chance to come back. But next time, Jane wanted a family.

She gathered her two bags as the plane taxied. Then, unsure of who might be greeting her, she dropped the luggage and walked to the bathroom for a quick look. The dark circles under her eyes told the tale of a weary person, and the one gray hair she'd acquired while in Stockholm screamed that she was a woman of accomplishment. Jane didn't mind. She'd earned it all.

When the hinged door swung open, the flight attendant stepped aside, gesturing for someone to come aboard. Instinctively, Jane took a step back, reaching behind her to search for her gun. After the incident in her apartment, she wasn't taking any chances.

He'd aged little; a silver fox who exercised a good skin routine. But when he took off his sunglasses, Dr. Peter Hudson was indeed showing signs of getting older. He smiled, and Jane felt herself choke up. And Jane didn't cry. Ever.

When she'd fled the United States, Matt Matthews was dead, and her relationship with NYPD counterterrorism officer Kelly Casey was in ruins. The last thing she'd said to him before leaving was, "Fuck you." He'd reciprocated in kind with an enthusiastic, "Fuck you, too."

Jane left for Stockholm, knowing only Peter and his husband, Matteo, knew her destination and intentions. Returning to the States after accomplishing precisely what she set out to do made her feel proud, at least for the moment.

"Dr. Dashwood, I presume?" he asked, opening his arms for a hug.

Jane lifted her chin. "Ellison."

Peter blinked his eyes with surprise. "No alias?"

"No," Jane said. "Once I got to Stockholm, I figured if someone knew who I really was, they were coming for me anyway. When I discovered my mother's identity, I finally had a name for myself, and I wanted to own it. I do, however, need to change my appearance."

"I think we can make that happen," Peter said.

She hugged him tight, and it was the first time Jane remembered embracing two people in the span of thirty-six hours. Jane wasn't a hugger.

He pulled away. "Let's go. We'll debrief in the car."

He held out a hand, offering to take Jane's bags, but she declined. "I'm out of practice," she said. "Not soft."

"Heaven help the idiot who would *ever* accuse you of being soft," Peter said with a sly smile.

When they made it into the back of the black limo, Jane took a breath, and Peter began a full-court press of questions.

"Why would they come after you? And who exactly do you think found you?"

Jane opened her leather satchel. "This arrived at my apartment," she said, placing the red book in his hands. "It can only mean one thing. Whoever is running Coywolf has found me. I killed Three without an order, and Kelly cleaned it up as best he could, but they knew. They *had* to know."

"Do you think Kelly blew your cover?"

Jane stared into Peter Hudson's eyes. Once upon a time, her bullshit meter was so accurate she could spot a lie like a dog smells a steak. Now, she wasn't so sure. If Kelly *did* rat her out, surely Peter would know. The question was, would Peter tell her?

Jane found herself quickly falling back into her old ways of mistrusting everyone she knew. Until she understood who was on her side, she'd play along. "No. I don't think Sergeant Casey blew my cover," she said with an inkling of a smile.

"*Captain* Casey," Peter corrected. "These days, he manages the entire NYPD Counterterrorism Bureau."

The smile faded from Jane's face. "How is he? Probably married with two-point-five kids by now, right?"

Peter shrugged. "He's in New York. I'm here. We don't keep in touch. I'm sure he's busy after the attack."

"Yeah," Jane said. "What do you know about that?"

"So far, only what the press has said; three suicide bombers. It was a coordinated attack on MTA under the Times Square Station. Rush hour."

"What about the senator. Maggie Thompson?"

Peter dropped his head to stare at his hands. "Yes. What a shame, too. She had such potential. I believe she could've been a future president. Now, we'll never know."

"Who's Wilbur Franklin?" Jane asked, casually moving on from the subject without sympathy.

Peter's expression shifted. "He's the new fron-trunner for president. Senator Thompson was his biggest competition until her campaign ran out of money. Why? You think there's a connection?"

Jane sighed, turning to look out the window.

"There's always a connection. You just have to know which dots to connect."

Peter returned the book to Jane, placing it in her lap before tapping his finger on the cover. "Connect this dot for me."

"Operation Thunderstruck. Ever heard of it?" she asked, briefly tearing her eyes away from the passing scenery.

"No. Enlighten me."

"I've been summoned. It's why I'm here, and by my best estimation, showing up to be a part of it will yield one of three things: either I'll do what they ask and pay my penance for killing Three. I'll be killed. Or both. The question is, in what order."

"Let me keep you safe, Jane," Peter said, touching her knee with his hand. "Let me, at the very least, do that for you. Matt would want me to. You know he would."

Jane looked at the brown backpack beside her. Inside was Matt's letter—a last goodbye from the man who'd sacrificed his life to save hers. She thought about it for only a moment before deciding Peter was right. Maybe she *could* do more from inside Maxtronix. Or was she unwittingly setting the whole place up to implode just by her very presence?

"Sure, Peter. I'd really appreciate staying with you and Matteo—or wherever you think I'll be the safest, at least until I understand more about why I'm here."

Peter smiled, then lowered the partition to the driver. "Stillwell," he barked, calling out the driver's name. "We're going to the house on the Potomac."

"Yes, sir," the driver replied.

Jane only knew of one house on the Potomac in

the Maxtronix real estate portfolio—the home of Christopher Matthews—Matt's deceased father. She turned to Peter, cocking her head in confusion.

"Don't give me that look. It's the safest place for you."

Jane took to staring out the window once more. She winced, knitting her shoulders at the idea of walking around Matt's childhood home. Jane didn't know if she was prepared to face the ghosts of her former life in the midst of seeking refuge, but decided she had no other choice. "Fine," she said. "I'll go to Potomac. Will I be all alone in that massive house?"

Peter's lips formed a tight, thin line. "Almost."

CAPTAIN KELLY CASEY closed the door to his office and leaned against it with a heavy breath. The past forty-eight hours were the worst of his career. Other than losing his parents and the one woman he'd ever loved, maybe the worst of his life. There were twelve dead New Yorkers on his watch—including a U.S. senator—and countless others injured. After hours of digging through rubble, coordinating with disaster task forces, the governor, the White House, and the senator from New York, Kelly had given at least ten interviews and a handful of press conferences where he spoke eloquently of the heinous attack and their quick response.

Now, all alone for the first time in a day, he uttered one word. "Fuck."

In the past seven years, he'd been able to assist in and even head up counter-terror attacks, with the public never the wiser. All of his triumphs were in secret, but his one loss was now international news.

He sat behind his desk, a steaming cup of coffee staring him in the face—no doubt left by Christina. When a knock sounded at his door, and it swung open unsolicited, he knew.

"Kelly?" Her voice was soft—feminine. "May I come in?"

Kelly let out an exhausted sigh. "Yeah."

Christina Templeton shut the door, clutching the doorknob with both hands behind her, a coy smirk playing on her lips. The daughter of Arthur Templeton, a powerful senator from New York, she was a striking blonde with more charisma than compassion. Kelly, who had been with her for just over nine months, enjoyed the perks—having her as arm candy and gaining an inside track with political pawns that dating the senator's daughter afforded him.

Aside from her beauty and her ability to sometimes please Kelly in bed, she failed to challenge him intellectually. Kelly surmised it was perhaps because her father was a politician, and she'd always been told what to say or how to think. This unquestioning obedience to her "daddy" gnawed at Kelly, getting under his skin to a point where he often had a difficult time hiding his genuine reactions.

Kelly Casey was a man of great strength, both in character and conviction. He had little patience for opinions born from blind conformity, always valuing authenticity and courage in others. Kelly never hesitated to do what was right or speak the truth, even when it was difficult. Deep down, he yearned for a partner who shared his unwavering sense of self, someone who could walk beside him with the same integrity and truth that defined his own life.

Now that extremists had finally succeeded in bombing the MTA, seven years after their first attempt was foiled, Kelly couldn't help but think of her. She had been the one who saved hundreds, maybe even thousands of lives back then. Now, when she crossed his mind, he couldn't shake the feeling that she might be watching from wherever she was in the world—seeing him as the failure he now believed himself to be.

"Are you okay, Kelly?" Christina's saccharine voice pulled him out of his own head and sleep-deprived stupor.

"What do *you* think?" He immediately regretted his curt tone and words.

Christina took a deep breath and exhaled. "I think you're grumpy."

"I'm tired and grumpy," he agreed, taking a sip of coffee before raising the paper cup to her. "Thank you for this."

Dolled up in a sundress and heels, Christina's appearance and cheerful demeanor were a stark contrast to how Kelly was feeling. He understood her heart was in the right place—she wanted to lift his spirits, remembering how he'd once said he loved seeing her in sundresses and a ponytail—but today wasn't the day, and he wasn't that guy.

"You know what?" Christina asked, her voice soft but loaded with implication. She walked toward him in slow, deliberate strides—the fabric of her dress whispering with every step.

"*What?*" Kelly's voice was tight as he clutched a stack of pink message slips. For all the NYPD's state-of-the-art technology, phone messages still came on paper—and he had a mountain of them to sift through.

"I came all the way downtown, dressed up just for you, and this is how you choose to behave? But it's fine, really," she added, a mocking sweetness coating her words. "I guess I shouldn't be surprised —it's not like you're ever concerned about anyone else, right, Kelly?"

Kelly's grip tightened on the pink papers. "I'm concerned about the people who died or were injured on my watch," he muttered, his gaze unfocused and fixed somewhere beyond Christina. "I need to work. I need to—"

Christina slipped behind his desk chair, resting her hands on his shoulders, fingers tracing small, teasing circles up his neck and into his thick red hair. "You need to unwind," she cooed, her voice dripping with suggestion. "And I think we both know how you like to do that."

Kelly shoved her hands away with a surge of raw frustration. "Christina, I know you mean well—" his voice cracked with the effort to stay calm, "but I can't do this right now. My mind is scattered in a million different directions, and I have work to do. There are dead bodies below Forty-Second Street that haven't been recovered yet. Did you know that?" His voice rose, anger biting through his words.

Christina blinked, feigning innocence. "I didn't come here to upset you," she said with an air of wounded pride. "I only came because I thought you could use some support. You know, a cheerleader... but if that's not what you want, I'll go. Clearly, I misread the situation."

"A *cheerleader*?" Kelly let out a harsh, bitter laugh. "You think I need a *cheerleader right now*? No one is cheering for me, Christina. I'm a total fucking failure. This happened on my watch. Do you understand?"

Christina's eyes narrowed, her tone turning cold as she moved toward the door. "You're being so selfish."

"Selfish? Are you listening to yourself?" Kelly wanted a fight. He *needed* someone to fight with him —to kick him in the ass and say, "*Yes, you're a fucking failure for not knowing about the coordinated plans to bomb MTA.*" But Christina would never be that person. She was good for dinner and a movie, for smiling and standing beside him at political and black-tie events. She only ever took him to task over his choice of shirt or drinking a beer when she thought he should've ordered something less pedestrian, like scotch. Holding him accountable for the big things—character or grace under pressure wasn't her thing. It never would be.

At the door, Christina paused, her hand hovering over the knob. "Kelly?" she asked, not bothering to turn around.

Kelly's cell phone rang, and he stood, pulling it from his front pocket with an irritated yank. "Hold on," he barked into the phone before removing it from his ear to look at her. "What is it?"

"I'll be at my place if you *actually* need…anything." Christina Templeton slipped out of his office, gently shutting the door behind her.

Kelly dropped his head back, staring at the ceiling in discontent. His frustration hung heavy in the air before he finally answered the call. "This is Kelly Casey."

"Captain Casey," the voice on the other end crackled through a bad connection. "I have information on a Jane Doe. Are you interested?"

Kelly paused, pulling the phone away briefly to check the blocked number. "You mean one of the victims?" he asked.

"No."

The unremarkable male voice had a distinctly Midwestern quality, marked by its clipped tones and the precise enunciation of every final consonant.

"Who is this?"

"No names."

"*Jane.*" Kelly said her name under his breath, his pulse quickening. He reached for the crisis management manual that never left his desk, the place where he kept the one and only image he had of her—an artist's sketch— carefully tucked between the pages. His fingers flipped through until he found it. Pausing, he opened the book wide, allowing himself a moment to trace the shape of her beautiful face with his finger.

"Where?" Kelly asked.

"There's a coffee shop next to the bookstore on the corner of Broadway and East Twelfth. One hour. I'll be wearing a red scarf."

DAY THREE | 1200 HOURS

As Peter and Jane approached the grand Matthews Estate on the Potomac, Jane instinctively turned her face away as they neared the imposing security gate. After a brief glance, the guard waved them through, and the driver eased the car onto the long, winding lane. Gradually, the sprawling mansion came into view, its massive façade looming at the end of the drive.

"How big *is* this place?" Jane asked.

"You've never been here?"

Jane shook her head. "I only knew of it."

"It's seven acres of heaven on the river," Peter said. "There are plenty of bedrooms—ten to be exact —and a couple of swimming pools if you're interested. There's also tennis courts and a horse barn; no one uses them, and the horses were sold off."

"And *why* do you believe I'll be safer here than in some dive motel?"

The car rolled to a stop, and Stillwell was opening Jane's door before Peter could respond.

"Besides the guards stationed around the estate," Peter said, "the house is secured with smart technology. Not even a squirrel could get off the grounds alive if it crossed the boundary at the wrong time. But, of course, feel free to leave and take to the road on your own if you'd like. My offer to keep you safe is fluid. You can walk out of here at any time."

"Easy, Peter," Jane said. "No innocent squirrels are dying on my watch, okay?"

Peter hesitated. "It's funny…you'll worry about an animal, but you don't think twice about taking a human life."

"I'd stop a human committing mass murder as surely as the sun rises," she said, slinging one of the bags over her shoulder. "But I'd never harm an innocent animal. The thing is, Peter, it's not always easy to tell the innocent from the *real* animals. That's why you have to pay attention."

"Okay, Jane," Peter said, placating her. "Grab your other bag. I've got a hairdresser coming in a half hour. That should give you enough time to shower and change your clothes."

Jane arched an eyebrow, casting a pointed look in his direction. "For someone claiming their proposal is fluid, you seem to have some pretty solid plans."

"Or don't shower," Peter said with a smile.

As she stood at the front door, her eyes were drawn to the sleek fingerprint scanner embedded in the stone—the sole means of entry into the home.

"Give it a go," Peter said. "Right hand."

"My fingerprint isn't in your database."

Peter smiled.

She pressed her right index finger to the pad, and the lock responded with a loud *click*, swinging the door open. "How?"

"Well, I hate to break it to you, but you left your

DNA and fingerprints lying about devil may care on your last mission. I lifted a print from a box Matt had with him the day he was…"

"Killed," Jane interrupted, her voice steamrolling through the tension. "You can say it, Peter. He was murdered—because of me."

Jane walked into the house, dropping her bags with a heavy thud in the front hallway.

"Hey," Peter said, gently squaring Jane's shoulders to face him. "Let me make one thing abundantly clear. Matt knew exactly what he was walking into that day. I know this because of the plans he set in motion beforehand. He was involved with the same crew you were working for. And like you, he believed he was helping people by aligning himself with the very monsters you were taking down."

"You weren't there, Peter," she said. "You couldn't understand."

Peter took a deep breath, steadying himself. "I *was* there, Jane. And I *do* understand. I saw everything. But that's a conversation for another time. Right now, we need to focus on who's trying to kill you and why. And who, or what, is Operation Thunderstruck."

"Sounds like a shit AC/DC tribute band to me."

Jane stiffened at the sound of the unfamiliar voice —an unfamiliar *British* voice.

"And this," Peter said, holding out his arm to present the young dark-haired man, "Is Silas Prince. Silas graduated from MIT, works for Maxtronix in R and D, and is one heck of an online hacker. He's also recently homeless, which is why he is here."

"You must be Jennifer Dashwood," he said, extending his hand to Jane for a handshake.

Jane took a step back, taking in the handsome twenty-something with blue eyes and a head full of floppy black curls. He looked more like a kid who'd rolled out of bed following an all-night grind session of Counter-Strike 2 and Red Bull than someone who worked Research and Development for Maxtronix. He was a Brit and a nerd—a handsome one, but a nerd all the same. It told Jane two things: he was unaware of his looks, *and,* in spite of his chiseled features, he'd probably had more sex via the Metaverse than in the flesh.

He seemed innocent enough, but Jane wasn't the trusting kind—a fact of which Peter was painfully aware. "Look, Peter," Jane said, picking up her bags one by one. "Maybe I *should* stay somewhere else."

Peter lowered his chin, his eyes locking onto Jane's with the stern disapproval of a father scolding a rebellious teenager. "Do you honestly believe I would allow anyone I didn't trust implicitly to work in Research and Development at Max HQ, let alone stay in the Potomac house?"

Jane shrugged. Given her past and the chaos of the last seventy-two hours, she could get on board with just about anything.

"Silas, this is Jane. Jane *Ellison.*"

Silas Prince tilted his head in confusion. "*Jane Ellison*? Then who is Jennifer Dashwood?"

Peter shook his head with chagrin.

"What?" Silas asked, deflecting his own blunder.

"*No,* Silas," Peter said, his tone firm and chastising.

"My apologies," Silas replied, feigning innocence. "It's just... I didn't scrape the dark web for a *Jane Ellison.*"

Jane stared the kid down. "Sorry to disappoint."

Hey," Silas said, tentatively stepping toward her. "I get it. I wouldn't trust me either—not without a complete digital footprint, some DNA, and a psychological profile. But sometimes, you've got to cut the coat according to your cloth. Right?"

Jane stared through him. She might've been out of the game for a few years, but her intuition was still spot on. She wanted to like the guy, which made her even more wary.

"Okay," Silas said, visibly uncomfortable under Jane's relentless glare. He took two steps up the main staircase before turning back. "I can see why Peter told me to stay out of your way. Just promise me you won't shoot, Kung Fu, or do anything to me that's gun-related or Kung Fu adjacent."

When Jane didn't respond, Silas continued his nervous ramblings. "See, I've been chatting online with this girl from Georgetown University—international relations major—and it's looking very promising indeed. My rizz is lit with this li'l bird, and it would be exceptionally hard to ask her to dinner if I'm dead or disabled in any way."

Jane shot him a withering, sarcastic glare. "I'm not big on promises."

A sly smirk crept across Silas's lips as he winked at Jane and pointed. When she didn't reciprocate his approval, he quickly climbed the stairs without looking back.

Peter watched Silas disappear to the second floor before breaking the silence. "Well, that went better than I expected. I didn't have the heart to tell the poor lad you're a Krav Maga master."

Jane turned to Peter and cocked her head. Her silent disapproval said everything she didn't.

"Okay," Peter said, throwing up his hands in surrender. "I get it. I should've warned you, but you should know Silas *wanted* to meet you. He's quite impressed with your, ah…*record*."

"*What?*" Jane snapped, letting Peter know she was less than happy anyone, let alone someone she'd only just met, had background information on her.

"If I had told you, you would've insisted on staying at some seedy roadside motel, and I can't keep an eye on you when you're off-grid."

"That's the whole point of being off-grid, *Dr. Hudson*."

"No, the point is, I want you here. I *need* you here. And let's be honest, *Dr. Ellison*—you need me too. As for Silas, if he's trustworthy enough to know Maxtronix trade secrets, he's trustworthy enough to know yours."

Jane inhaled deeply, letting out the breath along with the tension in her shoulders. She was tired, cranky, and in desperate need of a bed and eight solid hours of sleep. "Point me in the right direction. I need a shower and a nap."

Peter extended his arm, gently guiding Jane toward the west wing of the stately home. "I've arranged a room for you on the first floor with a terrace view," he said, his tone warm and accommodating. As they walked, he mumbled, "I know you like having an escape route."

"I heard that," Jane said, glancing inside each open door as they passed. She wasn't merely getting her bearings—she was mapping out the layout of the mansion in case she needed to exit under the cover of night—or Kung Fu Silas's British ass.

At the end of the hallway, Peter turned and opened a set of double doors, revealing a bedroom suite fit for a queen. Jane followed him through the ornate golden archway, past a stone fireplace and a small library filled floor to ceiling with books and picture frames. Some of the photos were black and white, others in color, but each time, the subject was the same—Matt Matthews.

Sunlight streamed through the French doors, catching the gleam of a single silver frame. Jane's gaze settled on a particularly striking photo of Matt in the desert, likely taken by a photojournalist. She found herself drawn to the image of the handsome man who saved her life. When she picked up the frame for a closer look, a knot formed in her stomach. Seven years and four thousand miles hadn't been enough time or distance between her and Matt's death.

Jane placed the frame back where she found it, then turned to Peter. "Please tell me this isn't his room."

"I would never do that to you," he said, gazing about as if each corner held a precious memory. "This was his mother's room. She died of cancer when Matt was twelve."

Peter took the bags from Jane's shoulders, placing them on the bench at the foot of the king-size canopy bed. "She would've liked you, Jane."

"Me?" Jane asked, eyeing the blue toile linens. "I'm sure the lovely Mrs. Matthews and I have nothing in common."

Peter furrowed his chin, causing his smirk to cock

to one side. "You might be surprised. Celia Matthews was beautiful, smart, and strong. She loved Matt with everything she had. When she passed, part of him died with her. After that, Matt lost what his mother treasured most—his spark. Chris wasn't much of a father after Celia was gone. He was more of a play-boy, really, with little to no time for Matt while he built on the empire his father started. Don't get me wrong—Matt had plenty of women in and out of his life."

Jane scoffed softly, dismissing the comment without a word, casting her eyes on the expensive rug beneath her feet.

"I never saw that spark again, Jane," Peter continued. "Not until he met you."

Jane lifted her eyes to Peter, the gravity of his words lingering in the air. Throughout her life, she'd borne more than her fair share of responsibility. As a child, she carried burdens that should've been shouldered by the adults around her. As a Marine, the lives of her comrades rested in her hands. And with each covert operation under Coywolf, she navigated dangers where countless lives unknowingly hinged on her decisions.

But Jane had never fully shouldered the profound responsibility of love. She had held lifeless bodies in her arms as their hearts stopped beating, but she had never cradled a man's heart with love—never held their trust and vulnerabilities as her own. Though she hadn't accepted it, Jane understood love transcended the thrill of passion; love was a profound duty, and the stewardship of another's soul was a responsibility she had yet to truly embrace.

"Don't say that, Peter."

"Why? I thought Jane Ellison only dealt in truths these days."

"You're not playing fair."

Peter walked to the door, lingering between the bedroom and the hallway. "Life's not fair, Jane," he said, turning to leave. "You of all people can appreciate that. Get some sleep. We'll talk after you've had a chance to rest and we start your makeover."

Jane glanced at her reflection in the fancy gold-leaf mirror directly in front of her. Twisting her ponytail, she wondered who she would become.

DAY THREE | 1300 HOURS

Kelly Casey looked at his watch and shut the door to his unmarked car. He still had two blocks to go before making it to the corner of Broadway and East 12th, but the side streets in the East Village gave him few parking options. When he finally reached the coffee shop, he scanned the room, looking for a red scarf. He found nothing.

Frustration built inside him as he wondered if he was chasing a ghost in the middle of the biggest crisis of his career. His shoulders sagged from a mix of fatigue and irritation. The line for coffee was short—just two people—so he ordered a double espresso, tipped the barista, and stepped aside. As he waited for his name to be called, he kept a sharp eye on the front door.

"Casey?" the barista called, nodding in Kelly's direction.

Kelly raised a finger and grabbed his coffee. As he glanced toward the back room, he noticed the anxious NYU students and wannabe novelists hunched over their laptops, each staking out a spot on the various couches and chairs. With one final scan of the room, Kelly turned to leave.

Sitting in a tiny nook by the shop's storefront window, he spotted a young man with brown hair and a baby face. Despite the patchy attempt at a beard, Kelly knew he was older than he looked. Draped over his black leather jacket was a scarlet-red scarf.

Their eyes met briefly before the man looked away. Kelly approached, taking the wooden chair across from the cushioned window seat. He didn't speak, only stared at the man in the red scarf.

"Nice to finally meet you."

Kelly's expression remained blank. Only after a cautious sip of his hot coffee did he speak. "*Finally*?"

The man regarded Kelly. Pulling a pen from the front pocket of his jacket, he picked up a napkin from a stack on the table near his scone and scribbled, *They've been watching you since she left.* "I've been watching your press conferences. My name is Levi Grant."

Kelly fought to keep his confusion hidden. "Reporter?"

Levi smirked. "Is it that obvious? I'm an investigative journalist with *Al Alami*, Captain Casey—the English platform."

Kelly took the napkin and the pen from Levi's hand, scribbling as he spoke. "I suppose you want a statement from me." *We're being recorded but not watched?*

Levi gave him a single nod. "It's the biggest terrorist attack on U.S. soil in over a decade, Captain Casey. How do you feel about it happening on your watch?"

Kelly's eyes narrowed into an irritated glare, his

lip curling. The tension in his face betrayed the simmering frustration beneath his calm demeanor. "How would *you* feel?" he asked, taking the pen from Levi's hand to write: *What's this about?* "I'm heartbroken. People lost their lives—their limbs. It's a horrible situation, but New Yorkers are strong. Off the record, *Levi,*" Kelly said, mocking his name, "New Yorkers don't just bounce back; we rise from the ashes stronger than before, and we live to see the day we bring our enemies to their knees."

Operation Thunderstruck. Jane Doe. Levi slid the napkin back across the table. "Can I quote you on that?"

Kelly raised a single brow. "I said *off the record.* "Look," he said, picking up the napkin to inspect it closely before turning it over to write: *Where is she?* "I'm a very busy man at the moment, Mr. Grant. Perhaps you can call my assistant, and we can set up a more convenient time to talk."

Levi took the napkin and wrote two words: *Matteo Caruso.*

Kelly saw the name and took a full breath, the relief evident on his face. Jane was in touch with Matteo, and that meant one thing: his friend, Peter Hudson would know how to reach her.

"I suppose I could manage that," Levi said. "As long as you don't renege on me."

Kelly took the napkin back, circling the words *Operation Thunderstruck.* "You have my word."

Levi nodded. "Good, because this is big. You know—national security big, Captain Casey. I can't imagine the Office of Homeland Security—or even the White House—making any decisions about New

York City's safety without collaborating closely with your office."

Kelly met Levi's gaze with a cold, unwavering stare—the kind that could rattle most men. But not Levi Grant. No, Levi looked as if he'd seen some shit, and it was only then Kelly noticed the dark circles under the journalist's eyes. "It's always a team effort," Kelly said.

Levi casually wadded up the napkin and left it on the table. Then, as he stood, he deliberately knocked over his coffee cup.

Kelly was quick to rise to his feet as Levi hurried to mop up the mess with the napkin, now soaked in coffee. The soppy brown paper, covered in their scribbled notes, began to disintegrate—the ink now merely a blur of liquid blue.

"Sorry about that," Levi said. "I caught my knee on the table leg."

"No problem."

"I'll be in touch with your assistant, Captain Casey," Levi added, giving Kelly a quick nod before walking out the door.

"I'll let her know to expect your call."

Kelly sat down at the table and watched Levi Grant walk away, hands in his pockets. If Levi was wearing a wire, who was it for? *Al Alami*? Operation Thunderstruck? Kelly hadn't seen or spoken to Jane in six years, but he knew the people she was associated with were never on the up and up. There was always something brewing beneath the surface—and it was never good. Jane lived in a world where trust didn't exist. And yet, once upon a time, she had trusted Kelly.

Jane broke his heart the night she slipped away,

vanishing into the darkness after their final argument without so much as a whispered goodbye. All she left behind was a brief letter—just a few empty lines saying she had to go, that she didn't know how to be in the kind of relationship he deserved. But Kelly knew better. He'd heard it countless times before—Jane insisting she wasn't capable of loving him completely. But deep down, Kelly understood it wasn't the truth that kept her from him—it was fear. Fear of vulnerability, of being hurt, of allowing herself to be truly seen.

The night she uncovered the truth about her mother—and realized who Kelly's parents had been to her as a child—Jane's walls crumbled. In that fleeting moment of helplessness, she didn't just allow the truth in; she let Kelly in too. He saw the depth of her pain, the scars she had hidden for so long, and for the first time, Kelly believed he was falling in love.

Since then, he had often accused Jane of ignoring what was real, of burying the truth beneath her need for control. She spent her entire life convinced no one could ever love her. But it was a lie. Kelly's parents loved Jane as if she were their own daughter. His father had searched for Baby Doe for years, never giving up hope. And now, Kelly loved her—with all her flaws, her scars, her brokenness. He loved her fiercely. And even though she might never believe it, he loved her still.

It wasn't until Jane discovered the shocking truth—that her biological father was Siad al Daleel ul Khyayraat, a notorious terrorist and mastermind behind countless attacks—that Kelly was able to do what his father couldn't: solve the mystery of Jane Doe's disappearance from public records.

Before he died, Kelly Casey's father had spoken at length about the covert operations of the United States Government—how they had the power to make anyone vanish and how he feared they were responsible for Baby Doe's disappearance. However, Kelly never fully understood the depth of his father's distress until *he* found Jane. She was the one woman who made him feel like the man he'd always aspired to be, yet at the same time, she could reduce him to a sensitive, heartbroken boy. When she vanished, Kelly became his father all over again—haunted by the fear that she'd been erased—just as they'd when she was a baby.

Jane left a deep, unhealed scar on Kelly's heart—one that refused to heal. He dreamed of her constantly, and in his waking hours, she invaded his thoughts even more. Every time he was with another woman, it was Jane he imagined in his arms. In his lonely moments, his mind always drifted back to her, aching to know where she was and what she was doing. Jane had been gone six years, but to Kelly, it felt like an eternity.

As he left the coffee shop and walked toward his car with renewed purpose, Kelly pulled his phone from his back pocket and made the call. If Peter Hudson and his husband Matteo Caruso knew where Jane was, Kelly was determined to find her—no matter the cost.

DAY THREE | 1500 HOURS

Jane tossed her head forward while Lance, from *Styles by Lance*, expertly blow-dried her freshly colored hair. He'd driven in from D.C. just for the occasion. The "mousy brown," as he'd called it with a sneer, was gone. Jane had been transformed into a vibrant redhead. She'd chosen the color herself when Lance offered her the choice between blonde and red. Subconsciously, she realized it might have been a way to honor the man she'd left behind—a realization that only struck her after the color was set.

"Give us a toss back, love," Lance said with a playful wink.

Jane did as she was told, slightly taken aback when she saw herself in the mirror.

"Sweetheart, it's been a minute, but I have to say, I'm impressed with how you've leveled up. Last time we met, you didn't give a shit about your hair, but now? Well, at least I can tell you've moved on from dollar-store shampoo."

Jane forced a smile. "Thank you?"

Lance ignored Jane's remark, too focused on running his fingers through her hair, scrunching and bunching the ends. "The keratin treatment seriously revived your parched tresses, and sweetie," he said, throwing a hand, "your natural color has latched onto this red like a desperate twink at a gay muscle bar. Honey, you were made to be a ginger."

Jane nodded. She didn't want to rain on Lance's parade by telling him she didn't care about the color of her hair. However, when he grabbed the curling wand and started going on about a "big idea" for "beach waves," Jane put her foot down.

"Lance," Peter said, walking into the bathroom with a knock. "She looks gorgeous."

Jane's expression remained impassive, like a calm sea without a ripple of emotion, while the gay men around her swam in their own compliments. "Beauty isn't an objective," Jane said. "I just need to be unrecognizable."

Lance patted himself on the back. "I love it when I'm this good. Sometimes I even surprise myself."

When Lance finished fussing with her hair—tossing and running his hands through it repeatedly—Silas arrived on the scene.

"Blimey, that color looks smashing, don't it?" Silas said, his polished English suddenly slipping into a cheeky Cockney lilt.

Jane's quick look in the mirror morphed into a steely stare. "Okay, that's enough," she said, yanking off the red cape Lance had draped around her. "I've changed my hair, and with any luck, I can keep a low profile for a bit."

Lance lowered his chin and gave her a pointed look from beneath his brows. "Sweetie, if you were trying to avoid attention, you should've stuck with the brown."

"Thank you for coming in today, Lance," Peter interjected quickly, stepping between Lance's comment and Jane's emerging snarl. "Let me show you out—now."

Jane brushed the remaining bits of hair from her shoulders and took a long, hard look in the mirror—something that didn't escape Silas's attention.

"It really does look nice, Jane. You look quite...*pretty*...actually."

She turned to face him; her expression unwavering. "Again, beauty isn't ab objective."

"An *objective*?" Silas said, barely stifling a laugh. "I don't think you can call it an *objective*. You either *are* attractive or you're *not*. And you are. It's all a game of chance in the DNA pool, actually."

Jane stared into his face, void of emotion. If he only knew her gene pool led directly to one of the world's deadliest killers, he might reconsider his stance on nature versus nurture. Sure, her mother, Dessa, was undeniably intelligent and beautiful—but those very traits might have been what attracted her vile father in the first place.

"You see," Silas continued, "with each generation we trace back, the amount of autosomal material you inherit from an ancestor is expected to halve. This genetic material gets passed down in chunks, and after about nine generations, it's likely that a specific ancestor contributed none of the autosomal material that makes you... well, you. You... and your blue eyes."

Jane was accustomed to intellectual heavyweights constantly bombarding her with their knowledge and opinions; she had spent six of the last seven years surrounded by some of the most brilliant and creative minds in the world. Yet with Silas, she couldn't quite tell if he was trying to impress her or if he simply couldn't help himself.

"I get your point, Silas," Jane said. "I'm just not sure what it has to do with me."

"Beauty is in the eye of the beholder, yes. But by any standard, you are a stunning woman. Peter tells me you could probably kick my teeth in, but that doesn't change the fact. And since it's said the apple doesn't fall far from the tree, I can only assume both of your parents were equally attractive. It makes sense—beauty attracts beauty."

The apple doesn't fall far from the tree. Silas's words echoed in Jane's mind, sending a chill through her. As her father's face flashed before her eyes, a cold dread began to coil around her, tightening with every beat of her heart.

She won't kill me. She can't kill her father. But Jane could. And Jane did. Now, she imagined Coywolf and Crow were hunting her. Operation Thunderstruck would most likely be her repentance—whether she wanted to pay or not.

"Look who's here."

Jane recognized the voice, but the face was unfamiliar. It wasn't until long after she had ended SDK's life that she realized Matteo Caruso was the man who had given her the information she needed to escape Coywolf with her life. When she asked him why, Matteo had simply said, "When I wanted out, someone helped me; it only felt right to return the favor."

Those words haunted Jane during her lonely

nights in Sweden. She had fled the United States without paying it forward. Perhaps Thunderstruck wasn't her penance—it was her second chance.

"Matteo," Jane said, acknowledging him with a subtle rise of her chin.

"The red suits you," he said with a warm smile.

Jane glanced around the room, feeling the eyes of every man fixed on her. For a woman accustomed to living in the shadows, their collective attention felt suffocating. "Well, that's done," she muttered, awkwardly edging out of the bathroom and into the bedroom. "There are some things I need to take care of." Her voice trailed off, the air around her heavy with unspoken tension.

"Things?" Peter asked, following her.

Jane nodded but didn't elaborate.

"Do you need a car?" he asked.

"If you can spare one."

"One?" Silas said with a sarcastic laugh. "There are like...*twenty* cars here."

Jane looked to Matteo and Peter, who both seemed visibly perturbed by Silas's confession.

"In the garage," Peter said. "Take the black Range Rover. The keys are in it."

Jane picked up her backpack and walked to the door.

"Before you go," Peter said. "I'd really like to show you some of the things we've been working on."

"Now?" she asked.

"I know you, Jane. When you walk out that door, who knows when I'll see you again.

She paused, taking a step toward Peter.

"Aha!" he exclaimed, a triumphant smile

spreading across his face. "I've got you. You need to know."

"Lead the way."

Jane followed Peter into an office that looked nothing like him. "This must've been old man Matthews' office, right?"

"Not my style?"

"No. I doubt it ever really suited Matt either."

"But it is a perfect place to lay low, my dear. A quiet spot to disappear and experiment with some new technology."

"I'm all ears, Dr. Hudson," Jane said, settling into a chair.

"When you were here last, we utilized some new technology."

"You mean the Mia V?" Jane asked.

"Exactly!"

"Don't tell me you've made them smaller," she said, the thought of sharing her own work in Stockholm with Peter briefly crossing her mind.

"We made them smarter. We enhanced their intelligence and programmed them with advanced facial recognition software. I'm eager to demonstrate it for you."

"You've developed facial recognition software?"

"We've refined the system significantly. It's currently undergoing testing at MIT, using the student population as a live dataset. We're debugging it by cross-referencing student IDs with CCTV footage to track their movements to and from classes in real time."

"And that's not an invasion of privacy?"

"Patriot Act," Peter said with a wink.

"Another advancement we've made is replacing

Tetrodotoxin with a compound we've engineered ourselves—"

"Maxtronitoxin?" Jane interrupted with a smile. She was intrigued but also apprehensive. Maxtronix could design and manufacture some of the most advanced bots in the world, but in the wrong hands, their potential for catastrophic misuse was undeniable and could prove disastrous.

"X-22," Peter said with wide-eyed excitement.

"What? It took twenty-two tries to get it right?"

"Maybe," he said, sitting back in his chair.

"What's the countermeasure for these weapons?" Jane asked.

"They could possibly be taken down with a green dazzler—you know, disorient them."

"But who carries a green laser with them everywhere they go, right?" Jane said, her tone light, though she was only half-joking.

"I do have something you can take with you to test," Peter said, opening the top drawer of his desk. He handed Jane what appeared to be an ordinary bobby pin.

"What does it do?"

"It emits invisible infrared light, so when you have it in your hair, any CCTV camera will only see a bright light and not a face."

"Now *this* one I can get behind," Jane said, tucking it into her hair behind her ear. "Anything else?"

"That's all for today," Peter said. "It's really good to see you again, Jane."

"It's good to be seen." Jane stood to leave, pausing at the door. "You know, Dr. Hudson, when we have a moment, I'd like to share some of the projects I've been working on."

"I'd like that very much."

Jane walked away, heading for the garage, her mind already processing the shift in Maxtronix's focus. It was clear that Peter Hudson had steered the company away from mass-scale destruction with drones capable of leveling entire towns to more covert operations. Maxtronix was no longer employing a shotgun approach to warfare but surgical precision.

"Jane," Peter said, stopping her. "Don't do anything stupid."

"Stupid?" she asked, turning back.

Peter's phone rang in his pocket, but he didn't rush to answer. "Come back when you're finished with…*whatever*," he said. "We need to talk more."

Jane gave him a curt nod before turning on her heel and headed back to the room. Standing at the foot of the bed, she paused at her leather satchel on the bench. As she dug inside, her hand hovered over Matt's scarf. Wrapping it around her neck, it felt as if she was deliberately torturing herself. His clothes. His house. It was emotional self-flagellation, and Jane knew she needed to leave. Thankfully, she did have somewhere she needed to go.

Navigating the long corridor from the guest room, she wound through the maze of hallways, always moving east—the direction Silas had said led to the garage. When she arrived, Silas's sarcasm became clear. More than twenty cars lined the space, including a sleek black limo and a new gleaming gray Bentley Flying Spur. On the far left sat a single black Range Rover SUV.

But something else caught Jane's eye. A classic 2001 BMW 740i—navy blue.

"*Matt*," she whispered, her voice breaking as his name caught in her throat.

She opened the passenger door of the BMW and slid into the front seat, the familiar scent of worn leather surrounding her. It was the same car he'd driven the night he'd shown up unannounced at her Atlanta apartment.

Jane inhaled deeply, closing her eyes as the memories flooded back, pulling her into a dark, hidden corner of her mind. She could almost see him beside her—the way he'd wrinkle his nose and squint his eyes whenever he told the truth—a truth he could never quite keep to himself, no matter how hard he tried. The image of him, so vivid and raw, caused her chest to tighten.

You think I'm a cupcake—that I'm soft. Don't you? Those were his words to her that first night. Back then, Jane had no idea just how tough Matt Matthews would prove to be. Now, the weight of his sacrifice was something she carried with her every single day.

As Jane shifted in the seat, ready to exit the car, something tucked under visor caught her eye. When she flipped it down, Matt's car keys tumbled into her lap.

"Well, if that's not a sign," she muttered to herself in disbelief. "I don't know what is."

Out of the car and into the driver's seat, Jane took a deep breath before turning the key in the ignition. After a few rhythmic clicks, the car let out a low growl as the engine struggled to catch before humming into a roar. She revved the motor, a thrill coursing through her veins as a huge smile crept across her face. Jane never imagined she would ever feel this close to Matt again, but here she was, surrounded by the echoes of his life.

As Jane sped out of the garage, she barely touched the brakes, offering a quick wave to the guard stationed at the security gate. The road to Langley, Virginia, stretched ahead of her. At the first red light, she turned on the stereo. The CD player whirred to life, and the familiar opening chords of "Jane" by Jefferson Starship filled the car.

She couldn't help but smile, amused by the coincidence. As the song reached the chorus, she found herself singling along.

The next track began, and she instantly recognized Stephen Tyler's raspy voice belting out "Janie's Got a Gun." Jane laughed out loud as she skipped ahead, only to be greeted by Rod Stewart's soulful wail of "Baby Jane." It was only then that Jane voiced what she already knew.

"You dork," she whispered with a huge smile. "You made a CD of Jane songs."

For a brief moment, Jane was completely absorbed in the music, her thoughts drifting back to Matt. The world around her faded, leaving her adrift in memories. But the blare of a horn from the car behind snapped her back to reality as she sat at a green light. Startled, she did her best to shake off thoughts of Matt Matthews and forced herself to refocus.

With a steady hand, she reached into the worn brown backpack on the passenger seat and pulled out the faded red copy of *Charlotte's Web*. Rule one of covert operations rattled in her head: *never tell the whole truth to anyone—not even those you trust.*

Jane had told Peter of Operation Thunderstruck, but what she failed to mention was the included coordinates hidden within the pages of E.B. White's classic novel. The mission was clear: report to an address in McLean, Virginia—one that Google Earth revealed to be a heavily restricted compound, nestled on ten acres just five minutes from the *Bubble*—home to the United States Central Intelligence Agency.

Kelly Casey sat in his idling car in the East Village, the hum of the engine barely registering over the turmoil in his mind. Interviews were lined up, and a briefing with the senator of New York loomed, but all of it faded into the background. All he could think about was her. With the phone pressed to his ear, he whispered desperately, "Pick up. Pick up. Pick up," as if willing him to answer would somehow work.

"Hudson."

"Dr. Peter Hudson," Kelly replied, his tone a firm declaration.

"Captain Casey. I'd ask how you're doing, but after the events of the past few days, I have an idea. How are you holding up?"

The tension in Kelly's shoulders coiled, burning through his muscles and radiating up to his ears. He wasn't much for small talk, nor did he want to rehash the details of the bombing. What he needed, more than anything, was to know if Peter had heard from Jane. As he white-knuckled the steering wheel, Kelly kept his voice steady, forcing a semblance of casualness into his tone. "It's been rough."

"I can only imagine," Peter said, his voice laced with genuine concern. "I know you're a very busy man, Captain—especially at the moment—so let me cut to the chase. What can I do for you?"

Kelly took a deep breath, trying to steady the nerves that threatened to betray him. He exhaled slowly, willing himself to stay composed. It took every ounce of control to even consider asking the question directly, so he didn't. They were both aware there were ears everywhere. If he was going to get any information, He'd have to choose his words carefully.

"We have a *Jane Doe*," Kelly began, his tone controlled. "I was wondering if your new facial recognition software, which I read about, might be of assistance."

It wasn't a lie. There was an unidentified female among the rubble at the Times Square MTA station, but she'd been positively identified earlier that morning.

"It's not something we usually do, Captain," Peter replied, his voice cautious. "The software is in beta testing on a controlled college campus. It's actually designed strictly for military applications—not for civilian use."

A heavy silence followed. Kelly struggled to maintain his patience, but the thought of Jane gnawed at him until he couldn't hold back any longer.

"But can you confirm that the software will work should I need to utilize it?"

Peter hesitated, and for a brief moment, Kelly wondered if he had pushed too hard. But then the answer came, poised and precise. "Yes, Captain Casey. It would indeed work."

Kelly exhaled slowly, loosening his death grip on the steering wheel. He glanced around before easing the car away from the curb. His department had already confirmed what he suspected all along—Reza Farhadi was behind the bombing. But what gnawed at Kelly was whether Jane knew the full extent of the truth. Did she realize the man she had spared—the one she'd marked with a chilling message for Siad al Daleel ul Khyayraat scrawled in Arabic across his forehead—was the mastermind behind the MTA bombings? It was the kind of revelation Kelly knew would bring Jane home.

Peter's silence on the other end of the line only fueled the frustration simmering beneath Kelly's stoic exterior. Jane was both his poison and antidote—the source of his deepest pain and the only cure for it. She tormented him, healed him, and kept him trapped in a relentless cycle of love and anguish. Despite all the suffering, he couldn't walk away. He needed her —more than he'd ever admit, even to himself.

"*Peter.*" Kelly's voice wavered, desperation bleeding through the controlled façade he'd struggled to maintain during the past few days. It was the first time he'd allowed his emotions to get the best of him. It was a crack in the armor he had worn for too many days.

"Listen, Captain Casey," Peter said in a measured tone. "If you find yourself hitting a wall, give me a call back. We'll see what we can do to help."

Kelly bit down hard on his bottom lip, the taste of blood threatening to break his resolve. He knew this was the moment to back away, to heed Peter's advice and let it go. But he couldn't. For nearly six years, Kelly Casey had waited, hoping for a sign, an email, a letter—anything that would tell him she was still out there. He told himself he just needed to know she was safe, but deep down, he knew there was more to what he was feeling. He wanted to tell her he was sorry, to say that he had never stopped loving her.

But Peter's advice didn't align with what he wanted at the moment—to speak with Jane. Both Peter and Maxtronix owed him—big. The mess with SDK, Matt, and Christopher Matthews hadn't cleaned itself up. Kelly was the one who'd smoothed things over with the city, the FBI, and the Secret Service.

"Perhaps it's time to collect on a favor you owe me, Dr. Hudson," Kelly said with quiet authority.

"Of course."

Kelly dropped his shoulders, a wave of relief washing over him.

"By the way," Peter added. "The last time I was in the city, I tried that new Chinese place you recommended in the Financial District—*The Jade Dragon*."

Kelly parked his car back at One Police Plaza in Lower Manhattan, taking a beat before the realization hit him. Peter was talking in code. "Glad you liked it, Dr. Hudson, but I've found that their dumplings are a little too *doughy* for me."

"I quite enjoyed the doughy dumplings," Peter said, subtly confirming they were discussing *Doe,* and not *dough*. "Captain, I need to hop on another call. I'll be in touch."

"Thanks for considering it, Dr. Hudson," Kelly said before hanging up and clenching the phone in his fist. He couldn't reach her—yet—but at least he knew Jane was safe for now.

When Kelly entered his office, he was met with an unexpected guest. Waiting for him, and making himself comfortable, was New York City native and United States Senator Arthur Templeton.

Kelly knew he was doing a shit job of hiding his utter surprise as he shook the senator's hand. "I'm sorry, sir," Kelly began. "It was my understanding our meeting was at your office in an hour."

Arthur gestured to the chair beside him. "Take a seat, son."

Kelly's heart sank. After enduring the worst two days of his career and learning that Jane was back in the States but still beyond his reach, he felt himself teetering on the edge. "What's going on?" he asked, forcing his voice to remain steady.

"I caught wind of something and I need confirmation from you," Arthur said, nodding for his Secret Service detail to step outside.

Rather than taking the seat offered, Kelly moved behind his desk, sitting in the executive chair as a subtle assertion of control. "I'll do my best," he replied, bracing himself.

"Several years ago, there was an incident in Queens—sarin gas. Do you remember the case I'm referring to?"

The memory of that chapter of his life with Jane flashed through his mind. "Yes, sir, I do."

"The way I understand it," Templeton began, leaning forward, "the tanks were wrapped inside carpets and stored in the basement of a known extremist."

"Yes, sir," Kelly said, keeping his voice steady.

"And on that very same day, when the FBI swooped in and seized everything, they found Reza

Farhadi in the basement of his rug store in Midtown, tied up with the name of Siad al Daleel ul Khyayraat scrawled across his forehead. Any of this ringing a bell?"

Kelly's jaw clenched, the tension radiating through his body. He had no idea where the senator was heading with this. "Yes, sir. I remember."

"And days later, this Siad Al Daleel ul Khyayraat —this SDK—turns up dead in a warehouse right off the Potomac River. But he wasn't alone. Weapons contractor and my personal friend, Christopher Matthews, and his son were found there too, both deceased."

"Yes, sir," Kelly repeated, his voice conveying no emotion.

"I find it rather intriguing," the senator continued, his eyes narrowing, "that the man who was supposedly tied up in his own rug store—a man who kept dozens of women imprisoned like animals in the basement of his shop—is the mastermind behind the attack in Times Square."

This time, Kelly only nodded. He knew what was next.

"Now I know *why* Farhadi had the opportunity to carry out this attack; my predecessor allowed him to be paroled from Rikers. But what puzzles me Captain Casey is why *your* name is all over the reports from that day. Why were *you* in Old Town Alexandria, on the Potomac River, on the morning SDK was murdered by—of all people—a journalist?"

Kelly had faced this question before, with the same accusatory tone, the same suspicion. Why *was* he—a member of the NYPD Counterterrorism Bureau—in Maryland? And how was he the only living witness to the death of SDK?

"Sir, if you've read those reports, then you know I was tracking SDK on my own time," Kelly said, his voice steady and firm with confidence. "I was on vacation when I got a tip from a source that SDK would be at a particular warehouse that morning. Was it smart to go there alone? No. Did I do it anyway? Yes. I didn't know if the source was reliable or not, so I took that chance."

Senator Templeton nodded slowly, his eyes locked on Kelly. "So, you're telling me you don't believe what happened in Times Square seventy-two hours ago has any connection to SDK's death or the sarin gas found in the basement in Queens—despite your fingerprints being at all three crime scenes? I find that hard to swallow, Captain. But if you *did* believe they were connected, surely you would have informed me long before a reporter from *The New York Times* dropped a bombshell theory in my lap."

Kelly wanted to stand up and shout *fuck!* as loud as he could. Instead, he remained calm, keeping his emotions in check. "I'm sorry you were blindsided, sir. The facts are, Farhadi, SDK, the sarin gas in Queens—they're all a part of the same extremist network. If I'd been given a heads-up and known Farhadi was released from Rikers for good behavior, I would've been on him like a hawk. But as you know, the right hand doesn't always know what the left is doing."

Senator Templeton shook his head slowly, skepticism etched into his furrowed brow. Kelly could see he wasn't buying the story, but the senator needed Kelly's support and cooperation to spin those very facts to the press. "This stinks, Kelly. It stinks to high heaven."

Tension twisted in Kelly's gut. "Yes, sir."

"I'm not going down in a fucking PR nightmare for this, son. I can and *will* cut you loose and feed you to the wolves if I have to."

Kelly had pissed off his girlfriend's father before, but this time the senator wasn't playing games. The threat was unmistakable. If any part of the reporter's story was verified and it led back to Kelly, he knew he would face the consequences alone. "I understand, sir."

The senator rose from his seat, and Kelly followed suit, offering him the kind of handshake and eye contact that confirmed all of their unspoken words. As the senator moved toward the door, he paused and turned back for a final word. "I'll see you tonight."

"*Tonight?*" Kelly echoed, momentarily thrown.

"The dinner," Senator Templeton reminded him. "Don't disappoint Christina."

The realization hit Kelly hard. In his sleep-deprived, Jane-obsessed state, he'd completely forgotten about the dinner—an event honoring the art achievements of New York City's public schools, a cause close to the senator's daughter's heart. "Yes," Kelly said, quickly recovering. "The dinner. We'll see you there."

"I thought about canceling," the senator admitted, "but we need to keep to business as usual as much as we can. We don't want those bastards to think they got to us."

"No, sir."

Kelly shut the door to his office and trudged back

to his desk. "What the hell?" he whispered, his frustration boiling over. He sank into his desk chair and dropped his head just as a knock sounded at the door.

Already on edge, Kelly snapped, his voice bursting with irritation. "What do you want?"

The door creaked open, and Kelly's secretary stepped in, her arms straining under the weight of two large paper grocery bags. "Sorry to disturb you, but you have a delivery from *The Jade Dragon.*"

"*What?*"

She nodded, struggling with the bags. "Where should I put all of this?"

"Anywhere," Kelly said, recalling his conversation with Peter.

She placed the bags on the small conference table in Kelly's office, then handed him a piece of paper. "Here's what's in the bags. The delivery guy said to make sure you got the order slip specifically."

Kelly waved her off, distracted by the list of Chinese takeout orders. "Sure, whatever. Thank you."

As Kelly stood over the bags, the rich aroma of soy sauce and red pepper wafted through the room. He glanced at the order form, then back at the bags. There were ten items listed. Kelly grabbed a pen and notepad, jotting down the numbers in the order they appeared on the handwritten slip.

A number nine, chicken with cashew nuts. A number one, chicken chow mein. Number seven, shrimp with mixed vegetables. Nine, one, seven. It was a New York exchange. When Kelly finished writing down the order of the menu items, he was staring at the phone number.

Kelly Casey smiled as he whispered one word: "Jane."

DAY THREE | 1700 HOURS

When Jane arrived, she wasn't entirely sure she'd reached the correct destination. The road, obscured by dense trees and thick brush, looked nothing like the entrance to a ten-acre estate tucked away in Langley, Virginia. But Jane wasn't one to turn back easily. With determination, she reached into her backpack and pulled out a Glock, placing it in her lap. She turned into the narrow lane with caution, the tires of the BMW crunching over acorns and snapping twigs. Keeping her speed below twenty miles per hour, she advanced slowly, acutely aware of everything around her.

Always alert. Always prepared.

When Jane reached the end of the narrow lane, she found herself at a dead end with no room to turn around. "Shit," she muttered under her breath, shifting the car into reverse to carefully back out of the tight space.

She had only gone about ten feet when, without warning, a twenty-foot-high chain-link fence, hidden beneath layers of camouflage and brush, began to slide open, revealing a hidden world on the other side.

Jane hesitated, her instincts warring with her curiosity. The old Jane would've charged in, ready to kill, but the new Jane knew better. She wanted to stay alive.

With one hand on the wheel and the other gripping her gun, she edged through the gate, alert to every movement around her. Ducking in the front seat, she craned her neck to peer out the windshield, noting the security cameras that dotted the landscape. There were eyes everywhere, but not a human soul to be found.

"What the hell have you gotten yourself into this time, girl?"

Another half-mile down the desolate lane, she spied a heavily guarded gate ahead, marking what seemed to be yet another dead end. Jane slowed the car but didn't come to a complete stop as the gates swung open, the MPs armed with AR-15s barely sparing her a glance.

Jane pulled up to the front of the stunning mansion, surrounded by perfectly manicured lawns and shrubs so precisely groomed it was as if a barber in East Harlem had given them a *High and Tight*. The site reminded Jane of another grand estate—Christopher Matthews' home on the Potomac. The manor was imposing and looked historical, yet it had the luxury of contemporary technology. Though it seemed to have expanded and modified over the years, the property retained its original stone charm, seamlessly blending the old with the new.

Jane put the car in park, taking the Glock from her lap and tucking it securely into the back waistband of her pants. She grabbed the heavy backpack from the seat beside her, then stepped out of Matt's car, making sure to lock it before making her way to the enormous front door. The gas lanterns flanking the entrance burned needlessly in the golden-hour light, casting long shadows across the stone path.

Jane rang the bell, rocking on her heels as a mixture of anticipation and dread settled over her. Was she here to be commended or condemned? *That* was the question.

The ancient door swung wide, revealing a stately gentleman dressed in a perfectly tailored black suit. "Good evening, Dr. Ellison. Right this way."

For a moment, Jane was taken aback by the use of her name and newly earned title, but she quickly shook it off. If they could track her down in Stockholm, it stood to reason they were aware of her academic pursuits as well.

Jane followed the man through the impressive entrance hall, the rich scent of polished wood and old books filling the air. He led her through a library lined with leather-bound volumes and into a beautifully appointed office. The walls were filled with tapestries that looked as if they were from the Civil War era, and the exposed stone looked ancient. It was a place obviously steeped in history, and Jane couldn't help but feel the gravity of the moment.

Logs popped and cracked in the massive fireplace to her right, the flames dancing up the original chimney that filled the entire wall.

To the left was a large desk, its counterpart, a tall, crimson leather chair, facing away. The butler gestured with an elegant hand toward a sofa positioned in the center of the room. "May I get you anything?" he asked.

"No. Thank you," Jane replied as her mind canvassed the room for possible escape routes. A set of French doors comprised the fourth wall, but the fifteen-foot hedge just beyond it obscured any view of what was on the other side. Jane took a seat, resigning herself to the grim possibility that she might draw her last breath in this room. It wasn't how she ever envisioned her life ending, but if this was it, so be it.

Without warning, the leather chair swiveled, revealing a small, gray-haired woman seated behind the desk. She was impeccably dressed in a cream worsted wool suit, with the only splash of color being a red silk scarf elegantly draped around her neck.

The two women regarded one another, each waiting for the other to speak. After a few moments of silent tension, the woman gave Jane a halfhearted smile. "Welcome to Bayberry. It's good to see you, Jane. How've you been?"

Jane's brows rose at the question as she struggled to place the woman. "I'm sorry. Have we met?"

The woman glanced down at a folder on her desk, then back up at Jane. "Years ago. I wouldn't expect you to remember. I handpicked you," she said, her voice filled with authority. "For Coywolf. My name is Wilhelmina Blackwood. Code name—"

"*Crow.*"

Jane echoed the word in unison with Blackwood, her breathy voice a product of her own astonishment.

Jane stared at Blackwood and forced herself to breathe slowly, gradually decreasing her heart rate. The silence between them was thick, and Jane's mind raced not with fear but uncertainty. She spoke her mind anyway. "Is this the end of the road for me?"

"End of the road?" Blackwood parroted.

"I disobeyed orders when I took out Number Three—SDK."

"I'm aware."

"I didn't say it because I thought you were unaware. I said it because it's the truth. I broke the rules of engagement. He wasn't mine to kill," Jane said, unburdening her conscience.

Blackwood closed her eyes, taking a deep and measured breath. "We did indeed have other plans for SDK—plans you disregarded when you decided to toss protocol out the window."

Jane held Blackwood's gaze, her voice steady and void of regret. "I wish I could say I'm sorry, ma'am. But to be perfectly honest, I'm not in the least. I don't know what kind of arrangement you had with him, but for me, it was personal." Jane looked down at her hands, a flicker of shame crossing her face.

"Again, I'm aware," Blackwood said, her tone now softer.

Jane's eyes darted up, filled with astonishment at the revelation. "You're aware of what, exactly?"

"SDK was more than Number Three to you," Blackwood said, steepling her hands on top of her desk. "He was your father."

Jane said nothing.

"He was the mastermind behind the bombing that killed Havis Monsour," Blackwood continued. "And soldiers loyal to his caliphate murdered Jennifer Drenkowski in Iraq, near Haditha."

"They wanted *me*. They believed Jennifer was *me*," Jane whispered. "It's my fault she's dead."

"Lance Corporal Drenkowski died because she was a soldier, and soldiers die," said Blackwood, her tone cold and matter-of-fact.

Jane took a full breath, her eyes fixated on the red silk scarf tied to perfection around Wilhelmina Blackwood's neck. Her eyes narrowed as she thought of Odile in Oslo. Maybe it was a coincidence, but if Jane had learned anything over the years, coincidence was merely rehearsed inevitability.

"Why am I here?" she asked, a newfound confidence hardening her voice. "Are you going to punish me? Kill me? Were you the one who tried to have me murdered in Stockholm?"

Blackwood lifted her chin, a slight scoff escaping her lips. "I knew where you were, of course. But I would never put out a public hit on you by someone who wasn't as well-trained as you. Surely you understand that much."

"So, you *did* send the assassin."

"I'd hardly call him an assassin," Blackwood said, a flicker of amusement playing on her otherwise composed face. "How difficult was it to render him defenseless and take him out?"

"What?" Jane asked, her irritation flaring.

"You heard me."

Jane took a beat. "It was a test?"

"I don't believe in tests. You're either worthy, or you're not."

"Look, if you've brought me here to eliminate me *privately*, then cut the bullshit. Let's get on with it," Jane said, stepping forward full of conviction.

Blackwood rocked forward in her chair, and once again she steepled her fingers atop her desk. "You're not here to be punished or taken out, Jane. You're smart, resourceful—maybe the best we've ever had. And even though you fucked me when you killed SDK, you're here because you're needed."

Jane crossed her arms, her irritation now fully visible. "Let me get this straight," she began, her tone laced with sarcasm. "You sent a hitman to eliminate me, and when he failed, *that's* when you decided to bring me back into the fold?"

Blackwood raised a skeptical brow. "There was only one way to get you out of Stockholm, and that was to reveal you'd been found. I needed you on the run. I needed you to come home. Besides, the man I sent to your apartment was a hitman *and* a rapist. You did me *and* society a favor when you snapped his neck."

"Great," Jane said, her disgust palpable. "Two for the price of one. Look, if you wanted me on your team, maybe the best approach would've been to shoot me straight."

Blackwood scoffed. "You've lost your edge, Jane."

"*What*?" she snapped, her anger flaring.

Blackwood tilted her head, narrowing her icy stare. "You should've realized long before now that Coywolf doesn't ask for permission—especially in the wake of a reckless decision such as eliminating SDK."

Jane squared her shoulders, ready for a fight. "With all due respect, I'd hardly call eliminating SKD reckless. I put a great deal of thought into ending the life of Three."

Blackwood's eyes glinted with darkness. "I'm sure you did. But it wasn't the plan handed down from the *Crown*."

"Crown" was code for none other than 1600 Pennsylvania Avenue—the White House. Jane assumed someone got their ass chewed out because of her imprudence, but only now did she realize it was Wilhelmina Blackwood—*Crow*.

"So," Blackwood began with a heavy breath. "Operation Thunderstruck."

"Is this an order?"

"I don't *ask*, Jane."

Jane took a beat and stepped away to reset her mind. Maybe she had lost her edge. Maybe she wasn't ready for what they had planned. Or maybe, just maybe, she'd been in hibernation. Like a bear waking from a long winter's sleep, she was slowly emerging from her protective cave. She might be a bit groggy, but she was no longer asleep. And with each moment that passed, Jane felt herself becoming awake. Wide awake.

"Unit 633 is an elite foreign operations group and splinter cell of the Taliban, tasked with conducting espionage, surveillance, and terrorist activities. They have settled nicely into the United States," Blackwood said, rattling off the information as casually as if she were reciting a grocery list. "They operate covertly, with its members blending into local populations, setting up sleeper cells, and conducting long-term surveillance in preparation for attacks. They're highly trained operatives with military experience and intelligence operations. They're well-versed in tradecraft, operate with a high degree of secrecy, and they're well-funded. One of their arms is planning something big. You would have carte blanche to do whatever you deem necessary."

As Blackwood turned away, answering a phone,

Jane eavesdropped. Her eidetic memory—one of the gifts she had always relied on—was still as sharp as ever. Jane could recall with vivid detail every image, sound, object, and word she'd ever encountered or read. Whatever had laid dormant in her mind for the past seven years was now wide awake.

"When?" Blackwood asked, her voice charged with urgency.

Jane stepped forward; her curiosity piqued.

"Who was supposed to be tracking him?"

Jane took another step forward, closing the distance between herself and Blackwood. Her eyes fell on the *Top Secret* folder lying on the desk, her name boldly emblazoned on the flap. Deep in her pocket, she felt her phone vibrating repeatedly—a call that would go unanswered

"Oh, for pity's sake, I'll take care of it myself," Blackwood snapped, her frustration palpable as she swiveled her chair and slammed the phone down onto the receiver.

"That didn't sound good," Jane said, a slight smile curling her lips.

"It wasn't." Blackwood rose from her chair and stepped around the desk, meeting Jane where she stood. "Are you armed?"

Jane hesitated, her mind racing as she weighed her response. When the pause lingered too long, and Blackwood's patience waned.

"It's a simple question, Jane. Are you *armed*?"

Jane locked eyes with the person who'd told her where to go and who to kill for more than three years. She had lived her life taking out terrorists one by one, and she'd never failed in a mission. "Of course, I'm armed. I was trained to be armed at all times. I have a gun tucked in the waistband of my pants, and a knife sharp enough to gut a bear tucked in my left boot. Is that armed enough for you...*Crow*?"

For a split second, the corner of Blackwood's mouth twitched in what Jane almost believed to be a smile. She knew it was likely the first and last time she'd ever see it.

"Good girl," Blackwood said. "I'm sending you to New York. *Now*."

"New York? What's going down?"

"We've intercepted some chatter. A high-ranking member of the House has been targeted by Liwa Al-Intiqam."

"Liwa Al-Intiqam," Jane repeated, the Arabic phrase rolling off her tongue with ease. "The Brigade of Vengeance?"

Blackwood tilted her head, obviously impressed with Jane's command of the language. "You're going to New York City—tonight."

Blackwood grabbed Jane by the arm, escorting her out of the room and down the hallway at a brisk pace. "Wait!" Jane shouted, digging in her heels. "I need to be briefed."

"We'll talk on the way," Blackwood shot back, her voice clipped and urgent. "But if we don't move now, we're going to miss it."

"Miss what?" Jane asked, lifting her head at the sound of a helicopter overhead.

"The suicide of the Speaker of the House."

Kelly Casey put his phone in speaker mode, placing it on the edge of the bathroom sink as he attempted to tie his black bow tie. Each time he dialed, the call went straight to voicemail, and with every failed attempt, his frustration mounted. Fumbling with the tie, he promptly hung up without leaving a message. She knew his phone number—of course she did. So why wasn't she picking up?

Kelly sighed, his blank stare fixed on his reflection in the mirror. The dark circles under his eyes betrayed the truth he was so desperately trying to conceal. "What the hell are you doing?" he muttered to himself. "She doesn't want to see you. Get that through your thick redhead skull."

"Did you say something?" Christina's voice pulled him from his own head as she breezed into the bathroom, wrapping her arms around Kelly's waist from behind. She peeked around his shoulder, shaking her head with a playful, sarcastic smile. "Here," she said, squeezing her petite frame between Kelly and the mirror. With a soft sigh, she gently took the tie from his grip, her perfectly polished nails brushing against his cleanly shaven face. "Let me."

Kelly lifted his chin, allowing her better access, while his eyes wandered back to the phone on the countertop. In the reflection, he watched as Christina meticulously adjusted the bowtie, shining him up for the evening ahead.

When she finished, she smoothed down the black satin lapels of his tuxedo and stepped back to admire her handiwork. "There," she said, satisfaction in her voice. "You're perfect."

When Kelly didn't reciprocate the compliment, Christina's smile faulted, her heavily lashed eyes dropping to the floor, revealing her obvious disappointment.

"'d better get going," Kelly said, slipping his phone into the front pocket of his jacket. "Your father already warned me not to be late—and not to disappoint you."

Christina looked up, searching his face, and when she finally caught his eye, Kelly could see the hurt in her expression.

"Car's waiting," she said, her tone barely masking her bruised emotions.

Kelly stared into Christina's eyes, guilt gnawing at him. She deserved far better than a man whose heart belonged to another woman—a woman he hadn't seen or heard from in six long years. A woman who, at this very moment, wasn't answering his calls.

He nodded, brushing a stray hair from Christina's elaborate updo, his touch lingering a moment longer than necessary. "You're too good for me, you know that, don't you?"

Christina's eyes sparkled with warmth, relishing

the rare compliment. Kelly didn't give them often, and he knew she treasured these brief glimpses of his approval. But then Kelly's phone rang, breaking the connection like shattered glass. In that instant, the importance of what truly mattered to Kelly Casey became painfully clear.

He fumbled for the phone, not bothering to check the number before answering. "Casey."

"Captain Casey, sir. I'm downstairs in the black sedan."

Kelly nodded to Christina. "We're on our way."

———

MATTEO CARUSO and Peter Hudson stepped onto the red carpet at the gala, pausing briefly as cameras flashed around them. Maxtronix was the proud sponsor of the NYPS Achievement in Arts Award for creativity in science, an initiative close to Peter's heart. In fact, Maxtronix supported nearly every major city's public-school arts awards, all a part of the vision Matt Matthews had laid out for the future of the company—nurturing the next generation of great minds. Tonight, the renowned Dr. Hudson would present college scholarships to two lucky recipients in what he referred to as "continuing their legacy of fostering talent and innovation."

Inside the doors of the Pierre, a luxury hotel on the Upper East Side, the Grand Ballroom was the epitome of opulence. It was a place where those who wouldn't dream of sending their children to public school had gathered, ready to open their checkbooks for the benefit of those who did—all in the name of the arts. The irony of it lingered in the air, alongside the disingenuous compliments they would exchange with practiced ease.

The Grand Ballroom was adorned with exquisite detailing, from ornate moldings to the floor-to-ceiling windows that offered breathtaking views of the city. Lavish floral arrangements graced every corner, while glittering crystal chandeliers cast a warm, radiant glow over the space, illuminating the room filled with Manhattan's elite.

Matteo leaned in to whisper in Peter's ear. "Looks like you've gone all out this year."

Peter nodded, his eyes sweeping over the crowd, half of whom he suspected had no idea why they were there. "What's the point of having money if you can't spread it around a little."

As Peter watched the high school teens file into the room—their ill-fitting suits and rented tuxedos a stark contrast to the opulence around them—he saw their eyes widen in awe. They were filled with the hope that one day, this world of luxury could be within their reach. It was exactly what Matt Matthews would've wanted—a chance for these young minds to dream beyond their circumstances, to envision a future where their aspirations knew no limits.

Kelly Casey's hand fell heavily on Peter Hudson's shoulder. "I was hoping I'd see you tonight," he said as Christina sidled up to the three men.

"Captain Casey," Peter said with a genuine smile. "How lovely to see you. How've you been?"

"I've had better days," Kelly replied, his voice tinged with exhaustion.

"Anything I can do to help?"

Kelly released a sharp, sarcastic laugh, tilting his

head back as if the ceiling might offer some kind of answer. Christina quickly took hold of his arm—a subtle but unmistakable cue to everyone that he needed to rein in his emotions. "I don't know," he replied, his voice laden with doubt. "Can you?"

Peter sidestepped the question, offering a polite smile instead. "Have a lovely evening," he said, directing his farewell toward Christina.

"You too, Dr. Hudson," Christina said. "And thank you again for your generous donation. You've truly helped make tonight special."

Peter lifted her hand to his lips, brushing a light kiss across her knuckles. "My pleasure. It should prove to be an exciting evening."

Christina nodded and smiled. Kelly stared into Peter's face—so many questions coming to mind.

"By the way," Kelly said, touching Peter's shoulder just as he was about to turn away. "Thank you for sending over lunch today. That was very...*thoughtful* of you."

Peter met Kelly's stare with a calm nod. "My pleasure. I know your people have been working around the clock. It was the least I could do to show my support." Shifting his attention to Matteo, Peter placed his hand on the small of his back. "We wish there was more we could do, but at this point, it's really up to you. You and your team."

"I'm sure you know even the smallest bit of help can make all the difference. In fact," Kelly said, turning toward Matteo. "Caruso, do you have a moment to chat?"

"I'm sorry, Captain Casey. Not tonight," Peter interjected, turning his back and taking Matteo with him. "We have guests to greet. Good Luck to you."

As Peter and Matteo walked away, Christina loosened her grip on Kelly. "You want to tell me what that was all about?" she asked, her forced smile barely masking her growing frustration.

"Not really," Kelly muttered, deliberately avoiding her gaze. All he wanted was to get Matteo Caruso alone. Five minutes. That's all he needed. That, and Jane's location.

"*Kelly.*" Her voice was tense, and her struggle to maintain composure was apparent. The cracks in her good-girl persona were beginning to show. "Look, I've been doing my very best to be supportive because I know you're under a lot of pressure. But can you at least *pretend* to care tonight?"

Kelly planted a quick kiss on the top of her head. "Go do your thing, Christina," he said, his mind focused on Matteo and his meeting earlier in the day at the coffee shop. "I can't stay late—too much to do at the office."

She pulled away, holding on to his hand until the last possible moment.

As soon as she was gone, Kelly turned on his heel, his only thought to distance himself from the crowd and the inevitable questions about the bombing investigation. He eyed the bar tucked away in the corner, suddenly finding the idea of a bourbon appealing—anything to quell his frustration and quiet his restless thoughts.

Kelly kept a quiet eye on everyone in the ballroom, but especially Matteo. He watched his every move. After his clandestine meeting with Levi Grant, Kelly was even more wary of the Italian husband of

Dr. Hudson. Something about him, aside from what he knew about Jane's whereabouts, nagged at Kelly —like an itch he couldn't quite scratch. Maybe it was Matteo's excessive involvement on Peter's behalf during the cleanup of the Matthews father-and-son meet the terrorists on the Potomac debacle. And Kelly wasn't alone in his suspicions. Mary Charles Madewell, his trusted friend and United States Secret Service officer, felt the same. Now, after meeting Levi Grant, he was confident his instincts were correct about him—he was hiding something.

Kelly approached the bar, catching the barkeep's eye, who acknowledged him with a confident chin-nod. "What can I get you?" he asked.

"Just a water."

"Only water, my man?"

Kelly nodded, and the bartender promptly pulled a cold bottle of Fiji from an ice chest, reaching for a glass to go with it.

"I'll just take the bottle," Kelly said, extending his hand.

The bartender hesitated, his eyes searching the room before landing on Christina and her committee friends, all gathered to congratulate each other on a job well done. "As much as I'd like to accommodate you, sir, I've been instructed that nothing leaves the bar unless it's in a glass."

Kelly's jaw tightened. "Seriously?"

The bartender didn't respond, simply sliding a glass toward Kelly along with a neatly placed cocktail napkin.

"Fine," Kelly said. He scanned the crowd, his eyes locking on Matteo Caruso, who was engrossed in a phone conversation. Kelly's interest was piqued when Matteo, looking visibly agitated, waved off Peter's attempt at affection.

Intrigued, Kelly edged closer as Matteo discreetly stepped away from the crowd to continue in private. Kelly wasn't the type of man who believed finding Jane would be as simple as being in the right place at the right time—like conveniently overhearing someone on the phone—but if Matteo was hiding her, Kelly needed to get close and listen.

As he ended the call, he seemed to scan the crowd for Peter, who'd already managed to navigate through the sea of people with his characteristic charm and grace.

"Everything alright, Matteo?" Kelly asked, appearing beside him without so much as a sound.

He flinched, irritation painting his face. "Damn it, Casey. Don't do that."

"Sorry, man. It just seemed like…well, you look like you got some bad news."

Matteo's gaze drifted across the room, deliberately avoiding eye contact with Kelly, dismissing him as if he were beneath his attention. "Quite frankly, Captain Casey, it's getting harder to tell the good from the bad anymore."

"Anything I can help with?" Kelly asked, his tone laced with feigned concern. He wasn't particularly keen on helping a man he didn't fully trust, but if it brought him closer to finding Jane, he was willing to play the part.

Matteo finally met Kelly's stare; his expression unreadable. "I can't find Peter in the crowd. When you see him, tell him I had to tend to something."

"*Tend* to something? What's going on?"

"Just *tell him*," Matteo said before walking away.

Kelly made his decision in an instant. Without a second thought, he slipped out of the ballroom and quietly trailed Matteo Caruso down the hallway and out the front door. He watched as Matteo climbed into a sleek black sedan, the driver barely waiting for the door to close before speeding away from the curb at 61st and 5th Avenue—tires squealing as they vanished into the night.

"Shit," Kelly muttered, his heart pounding. Determined not to let Matteo out of his sight, he eyed the brigade of NYPD squad cars parked in front of the hotel. Flashing his badge at a uniformed officer, he barked an order before jumping into a cruiser.

Kelly blew through an intersection on red, keeping the lights and siren off as he tailed Matteo's sedan, his focus razor-sharp. The NYPD insignia on the side of the car was conspicuous enough—he didn't need to draw more attention. "Where the hell are you going, Matteo?" Kelly said, one hand gripping the wheel, the other tightening around the radio.

He lifted the mic to his mouth, thumb hovering over the PTT button, but changed his mind. Calling it in would alert every beat cop on duty, and the last thing he needed was to ignite a wildfire of rumors about the head of counterterrorism commandeering a cruiser.

Instead, Kelly pulled out his phone and dialed his office directly.

"CTB," answered the woman with a distinct lack of enthusiasm.

"This is Captain Casey," he said, the tension building in his voice.

"Good evening, sir," she said, her tone instantly shifting. "How may I assist you?"

"I've commandeered Alpha Seventy-seven in pursuit of a possible suspect. I don't need backup—I repeat, I do *not* need backup. Keep this off the radio. Just inform Seventy-seven that I *do* have their squad car, and I *will* return it."

"Ten-four, Captain. I will make that call now."

Kelly didn't say goodbye but hung up and quickly changed lanes to keep the black sedan in sight. "Where are you going?"

The black car cut through Central Park, and Kelly trailed it, keeping at least one vehicle between them. He'd already committed the license plate to memory, just in case he lost them in the sea of black sedans that flooded Manhattan at night.

The police radio crackled with constant chatter, but one transmission cut through the static. "Three hundred, Central Park West. The El Dorado."

Kelly's pulse quickened. The El Dorado—a historic co-op on the Upper West Side—had housed countless celebrities over the years, from Marilyn Monroe to Bono. Much to Kelly's surprise, Matteo seemed to be heading in that very direction. As the car pulled up at Central Park West and 90th Street, Matteo was out and running into the building before Kelly could blink.

Sirens wailed in the distance as the dispatcher's voice cut through the chaos, repeating the address—this time with a name: Martin Pearl. The United States Speaker of the House. Kelly realized; this wasn't about Jane.

Kelly slammed the squad car into park, threw on the lights, and grabbed a radio before charging into the building.

"Matteo!" he shouted, his voice echoing off the marble floors of the foyer.

But Matteo Caruso didn't slow down. He sprinted toward the elevator, jabbing the button repeatedly with a trembling hand. The doors began to close just as Kelly reached them. Fueled by adrenaline, he lunged forward, and they shuddered open. Kelly stepped inside, his eyes locked on Matteo.

"What the fuck are you doing!" Matteo shouted, his face twisting in anger.

The elevator doors sealed, trapping the two men in the confined space. Kelly didn't flinch. He stepped nose to nose with Matteo, his voice a low, dangerous growl. "No, Matteo. What the fuck are *you* doing?" Kelly ground the question through his clenched teeth. "I haven't trusted you since you poked your nose into my business after Matt and Christopher Matthews died alongside two known terrorists, including SDK. And now, seventy-two hours ago, a man tied to those same terrorists managed to kill twelve people in *my* city.

"Why did you rush out of the party tonight and come here? Tell me. *Now*."

For three days, Kelly had sifted through the smoldering wreckage beneath Times Square, the devastation still etched in his mind. Dozens of people were injured and twelve dead—including a senator. If Matteo knew something about the bombing, Kelly was going to drag it out of him by any means necessary.

Matteo's silence was the green light Kelly needed. In a flash, he grabbed Matteo by the lapels of his tuxedo, yanking him close. Matteo's was solidly built, but Kelly was a force of nature—a brutish wall of muscle and relentless determination.

"Talk," Kelly demanded.

Matteo's expression hardened. "I have a job to do here, Casey. A job that doesn't involve you." His hand moved swiftly, and suddenly, a gun was pressed against Kelly's side, the cold barrel digging into his ribs. "Now let go of me," Matteo hissed, "before I'm forced to shoot you in this godforsaken elevator."

Kelly reluctantly released his grip, but not before giving Matteo a final shove that sent him staggering back, nearly losing his balance.

The elevator chimed as it reached the twenty-ninth floor, the doors sliding open with a soft hiss. Matteo bolted out, and Kelly was right on his heels, matching him stride for stride down the dimly lit hallway of the El Dorado.

At the end of the corridor, Matteo stopped abruptly in front of a door, his fingers flying over the digital keypad with practiced precision. Kelly watched, a frown creasing his brow—how the hell did Matteo know the code?

Before Kelly could voice his suspicion, the radio on his belt crackled, the dispatcher repeating the El Dorado's address. Matteo turned, his eyes dark with warning. "Call off your dogs."

"What?"

"Keep your men out of here. Call them off."

"Why the hell would I do that?"

"Because Martin Pearl's life depends on it. And whatever happens in here, you didn't see a thing. Understood?"

DAY FOUR | 1945 HOURS

Jane slipped through the delivery dock, her movements precise and deliberate as she infiltrated the ancient apartment building. The infrared bobby pin was secure in her hair, but she avoided the cameras wherever possible. To remain completely undetected, she knew she'd have to take the stairs—all twenty-nine floors.

Her pace was relentless as she ascended, every step a testament to the rigorous training she'd maintained in Stockholm. Jane's heart pounded in sync with her rapid climb, but she knew her conditioning wouldn't fail her now. By the time she reached the twenty-seventh floor, her breath was coming fast, but she paused only briefly, checking her watch. Blackwood's intel had been clear—time was running out.

With renewed urgency, Jane pushed herself up the final two floors, every second ticking away like a bomb in her mind. She arrived at her destination, her breathing heavy but controlled, her focus laser-sharp. She carefully entered the code she'd been given, the tension palpable as she quietly unlocked the door to the luxurious apartment on the Upper West Side of Manhattan. This was it—no room for error.

The home was shrouded in darkness, save for a faint light glowing from the bedroom. Jane's mind flashed back to the layout Blackwood had shown her on the chopper ride from Langley. The military CH-47F Chinook had made the trip to Manhattan in under an hour, landing on the Mount Sinai Hospital helipad with special clearance from the FBI.

Jane moved like a shadow across the main living room, her eyes sweeping the space. Antiques and accolades filled the room, a testament to Martin Pearl's life. The faces of his family stared down at her from photos displayed on every wall, silent witnesses to what was about to unfold.

As Jane neared the lone source of light, her pulse raced, but her breathing remained steady. She approached the bedroom, its faint glow casting strange shadows in the darkened hall. She paused at the crack in the door, holding her breath as she peered inside, every sense on high alert. Sweat beaded on her forehead, dripping to the floor in tiny puddles at her feet. Time was slipping away, and she knew the next few moments would determine the fate of Martin Pearl.

There he was—Tariq Maski, Number Five on *The List*. Dressed in tactical gear, a noose in hand, he was unlike any target she'd encountered before. Jane's eyes narrowed as she observed him checking his phone, where detailed plans were displayed. They were getting more organized. Jane didn't yet fully understand who was behind Liwa Al-Intiqam, but it was clear they had elevated their game well beyond the abilities of the group led by Three.

Improvise. Adapt. Overcome.

Without a sound, Jane drew a syringe from the pocket of her hoodie, her plan clear: drug Five into submission rather than kill him—at least for now. Jane not only wanted, but needed answers. She needed to know where his orders were originating— if she could get it out of him.

Through the narrow crack in the door, she watched Five work with cold, calculated efficiency. On the floor, Martin Pearl—the Speaker of the United States House of Representatives and one of the most powerful men in America—was reduced to a trembling, weeping shell of a man. Stripped down to his underwear, duct tape covered his mouth, and zip ties bit into his wrists and ankles.

Jane watched the scene unfold; every muscle in her body tensed as she calculated the optimal moment to strike. Attacking Five while his hands were free would be reckless. She had to wait—to bide her time until he was fully absorbed in the grim task of staging Martin Pearl's suicide.

Jane observed calmly as Five forced Pearl onto a wooden chair, slipping the noose around his neck. She felt no urgency or fear, only a curated readiness she'd honed over her years of training and countless successful missions.

Five tossed the rope over an exposed beam, hoisting the Speaker off his feet. Pearl's toes balanced precariously on the chair, teetering on the edge of life and death. Jane knew her moment had come. As the chair wobbled beneath him, Martin Pearl's eyes widened in terror.

Without a sound, Jane slipped into the room, moving like a shadow in the darkness.

Pearl's gaze met hers, a mix of desperation and

hope flickering in his eyes. Jane pressed a finger to her lips, signaling for silence. Pearl squeezed his eyes shut, tears streaming down his face as he awaited his fate.

Jane was a ghost—her steps silent and deliberate as she approached the killer from behind.

Five turned just as the needle bit into his skin, a brief flash of realization in his eyes. He instinctively reached for his gun, then the knife at his side, but it was too late. The near-lethal dose of succinylcholine coursed through his veins, robbing him of all control. Jane stepped back, drawing her own gun as she watched him slowly succumb, his body betraying him as it shut down.

As Five crumpled to the ground, he knocked the chair out from under Speaker Pearl, and the rope snapped taut, suspending Pearl from the rafter, his life literally hanging in the balance.

With lightning reflexes, Jane yanked the knife from Five's tactical jacket, her eyes catching the ominous glint of a grenade nestled in one of his pockets —a lethal surprise she hadn't anticipated.

Martin Pearl's life was slipping away, the noose tightening around his neck as his bound legs flailed like a fish out of water. Jane placed the chair under him, climbing onto it as his toenails scraped against the wood. The sickening sound of his struggle echoed in her ear as he fought for his life.

With two swift cuts, Jane severed the rope, and Martin Pearl crashed to the floor with a heavy thud. Jane caught him as best she could, easing his fall before immediately working to loosen the noose around his neck. She ripped the tape from his mouth, the adhesive tearing away with a brutal snap.

Pearl gasped for breath, collapsing forward, his lungs heaving as he stared at Jane with wide, terrified eyes—spittle falling from his lips as he sputtered and coughed.

"Thank you," he choked out, his voice trembling with adrenaline.

Jane sliced through the zip ties binding his wrists and ankles. The moment Martin Pearl was free, she turned her attention back to Five. His pulse was faint, his breathing shallow—each labored inhale a struggle against the paralysis creeping through his body.

Jane rifled through Five's vest with practiced efficiency, searching for anything useful. Her fingers brushed against a silencer, and she quickly pocketed it along with his Glock lying nearby.

Across the room, Martin Pearl huddled in the corner, his body wracked with uncontrollable sobs. He'd seen Jane's face—a complication she hadn't anticipated, but there was no turning back now. Her mind raced, her primary concern avoiding further identification by anyone else who might be watching.

Her eyes darted around the room, scanning for any hidden devices or cameras. She barely had intel, and she hadn't had to opportunity to plan. The idea of being compromised, of being made, caused her blood to run cold.

Suddenly, a faint creak echoed from beyond the bedroom door. Jane froze. She signaled Martin Pearl to quiet his blubbering sobs, her eyes narrowing as she moved swiftly and silently.

Positioning herself behind the door, Jane prepared for the unknown threat approaching. Whoever was about to fuck up her kill zone was in for a brutal surprise. With deadly precision, she deftly assembled the silencer onto the gun, her movements fluid, her nerves steeled for whatever came next.

The door swung open, and two men stepped inside, their backs to her. The moment they crossed the threshold, Jane cocked the gun, her finger steady on the trigger.

But as the men turned to face her, Jane's breath caught in her throat, the shock paralyzing her for a split second.

"Jesus, lady." Martin Pearl said, his voice trembling from the corner. "Who are you anyway?"

Kelly Casey's eyes widened, disbelief etched into every line of his face. "Jane," he whispered, his voice a stunned breath. "Jane Doe."

DAY FOUR | 2030 HOURS

Jane took a deep breath, forcing her heart rate to steady. Her nostrils flared as she inhaled, locking eyes with Kelly Casey.

Kelly followed suit, lowering his gun and taking a cautious step toward her. The longing in his eyes was unmistakable—he wanted to embrace her, to close the gap that years had carved between them. Jane could see it on his face. But what she couldn't understand was why Matteo Caruso and Kelly Casey were both at her assigned kill.

Without a word, Jane allowed the gun to slip from her grasp before crossing the room to check Five's pulse. Kelly stood on her perimeter; his feet rooted to the ground as Jane forced herself to stay in the zone. Meanwhile, Matteo took it upon himself to check on the Speaker of the House, who remained huddled in the corner. Jane had saved his life, but beyond that, she felt no need to engage with him. Not yet.

"Jane," Kelly called softly, keeping his distance, "what are you doing here? Where have you been?"

Jane lifted her eyes from Five's body, her attention quickly shifting to Matteo across the room. "What the hell are *you* doing here?"

"Duty called," Matteo replied with a shrug.

It wasn't the explanation Jane wanted, but it was one she understood. Why he'd brought Kelly Casey with him was beyond her. "Look," she said, her tone firm. "We don't have much time." Rising from Five's body, Jane approached Speaker Pearl. "Sir, you're not going to like what I'm about to say."

"Whaaa?" the Speaker mumbled, his voice shaking as he looked up from the expensive alpaca blanket draped around his shoulders. Jane nearly laughed at the irony. Even in the face of terror, the wealthy were wrapped in luxury, while most victims would be handed a scratchy wool blanket from the trunk of a random patrol car.

"Mr. Speaker," Jane said, keeping her head down. "We're going to need to stage this room to make it appear as if you did, in fact, commit suicide tonight."

"What are you saying?" he asked, his voice quivering.

Jane paused, her eyes landing on a photo of Pearl with his wife and two daughters at the beach. She picked it up and thrust it into his hands. "These people," she said firmly.

"My family?" he asked, looking up with the eyes of a desperate man.

Jane nodded. "They will be informed tonight that you committed suicide."

"What?" he nearly shrieked, now somewhat back to his former self. "Why would I do that?"

"To keep your family safe, sir. A powerful group of terrorists wanted you dead, and instead of killing you outright, they wanted it to look like a suicide. It's best if you let them."

"Duct tape and zip ties?" Kelly asked, picking up the evidence in his gloved hand. "The medical examiner would pick up on that right away."

"I said they were terrorists," Jane replied. "I didn't say they were smart."

"I need to call dispatch and keep officers from coming up here," Kelly said. "I heard the address over the radio. Not to mention I have a cruiser on the street."

"Make the call," Jane said, obviously perturbed. "And stop fucking up my one-horse parade."

Kelly walked away, barking orders on his radio, saying, 'All units clear. Situation is secure. No further assistance needed.'

"What about *him*?" Martin said, pointing at Five.

"Don't worry, we're not going to hear a peep out of *him*, and I'll clear the scene."

Kelly stood in the corner, taking it all in. "What's next?" he asked, causing both Jane and Matteo to turn. "I've cleared the scene. What I'm asking is, who knows you're here?"

Jane stepped up to Kelly, standing toe to toe. She could see the torment in his eyes—the longing. Even though she'd put six years and an ocean between them, Jane knew Kelly Casey like the back of her own hand. Without shame, he wore his emotions on his face while Jane remained steadfast in her mission. At present, she wasn't trying to spare the feelings of Kelly Casey but the life of the Speaker of the House —and *that* she had accomplished.

Still, she answered his question without emotion.

"Who knows we're here?" she asked, repeating the question. "So far, *you.*"

"Wait a damn minute," Martin Pearl said, piping up, finally finding his balls and voice. "I'm not going to tell my wife and daughters I'm dead. I've been traumatized enough; I won't put them through the same thing. I'll pretend if that's what I need to do—but I need to talk to Washington first."

Jane moved deliberately toward the Speaker of the House. "With all due respect, sir. Who do you think sent us?"

Jane crossed the room, brushing past Matteo before leaning down to check on Five's pulse rate. "I'm going to need *you,*" she said, pointing to Matteo, "to take him to a secure location."

"Kelly," Jane said, "you'll need to call Speaker Pearl's family and break the bad news."

"You can't do that!" Pearl shouted.

Jane locked eyes with him, her steely, unflinching stare sharp enough to make anyone's blood run cold. "Sir, these aren't just killers. They're the kind of people who will target what you love most. They'll rape and murder your wife and daughters—and if you're lucky, they won't film it. Am I clear?"

"I need to speak with Homeland Security," Pearl said, wagging his finger at Jane.

"Sir, I strongly suggest you follow our instructions. It's the best way to keep you and your loved ones safe," Jane said, doubling down.

"Why am *I* informing his family?" Kelly asked.

"Because you're the damn leader of the Counterterrorism Bureau in New York City, that's why. We need whoever's behind this attack to believe they succeeded," Jane said with contempt. "At least until I can hunt down the beast behind it."

"You can't just go around faking people's deaths," Pearl said.

Jane stared at him for a long, hard moment. Could the Speaker of the House really be so naive? In Washington, D.C., any scenario could and *had* taken place in American politics. With enough money and power, you could get away with murder—a *real* murder. "Sir, I assure you I *can* and *will* fake your death. Now, we don't have time to debate. Get him out of here," Jane said, issuing orders to a stone-faced Matteo. "There's a van waiting outside the loading dock with a gurney and body bag."

"*Jane*," Kelly said, bringing his voice down. "What about the medical examiner? What if his wife wants to see the body?"

"Yes!" Pearl shouted, pointing at Kelly. "Yes, to everything he just said."

Jane hung her hands on her hips and stared at the floor in frustration. "And this is why I work alone," she muttered. Lifting her head, she fixed her stare on Matteo. "Get him out of here, *now*. Kelly, *you* get the wheels rolling on any paperwork that needs to be forged."

She paused, glancing over at Tariq Maski—Five —barely breathing on the floor. "I need to tie up my own loose end."

Matteo paused at the door before leaving. "Mr. Speaker, you can leave in whatever clothes you have on your back. We'll get you something to wear when we arrive at a safe house."

"I don't like this," Martin said. "But if it's the only way, then—"

Jane cut him off. "It is." She'd had enough chitchat for the night.

With Matteo gone, Martin Pearl walked into his closet to put on pants, a shirt, and shoes. On the way, he picked up his phone from the nightstand, only to have Jane grip him by the wrist. "The phone stays here. Sorry."

An angry sigh escaped the Speaker's lips as he went back into the walk-in closet.

"Listen," Jane said, her tone softening as she made her way to Kelly. "I need to ask you something."

Kelly's eyes lit up as he closed the distance between them. "I want to talk to you, too," he said, lowering his voice to the deep timbre he knew turned Jane on. "By the way, I like the red hair. It suits you."

Jane shrugged. "Whatever."

"*Whatever*?" he echoed, devastation lurking behind his eyes. "Can I at least hug you?"

Jane shrugged again, indifferent.

Kelly stepped closer, gently wrapping her in his arms, his hands finding a familiar place around her waist. He pressed his nose into the curve of her shoulder, inhaling deeply, but Jane pulled away, peeling Kelly off her body.

Dropping his arms to his sides, he cocked his head as if trying to read her thoughts. "Tell me what to do, Jane. Whatever you say."

Jane stared into his eyes, finally blinking. "I need you to get me some heroin off the street."

Kelly blanched. "*That's* what you want from me? Heroin?"

"Or coke—as long as it's laced with fentanyl."

Kelly looked at the would-be killer lying on the

floor, then back at Jane. He swallowed hard. "I'm not really dressed for a visit to a trap house, Jane."

"Well, it was worth a try." She turned away, pulling her backpack over her shoulders.

"Where are you going?"

"To do what you can't. Tell Matteo I'll catch up with him later."

As Jane started to walk away, Kelly reached out and grabbed her arm, his firm grip enough to stop her in her tracks. "Why are you acting like this?" he demanded, his voice a mix of confusion and desperation.

"Like *this*?"

"Why are you acting like we didn't once have a life together? A beautiful life you walked away from."

"Just because I left doesn't mean I'm the one who walked away." Jane's eyes darted from the large hand clamped around her arm to Kelly's face, her stare intense and filled with unspoken words.

He released her, but before she could reach the door, his footsteps echoed across the room. "Wait!" It was the plea of a desperate but determined man.

Jane turned to face him, her gaze steady and unyielding.

"I'll get you the drugs."

"Tonight?"

Kelly nodded. "Tonight."

Matteo brushed past them with the gurney and body bag. "Is he ready?"

"He's in the bedroom," Jane replied, her voice detached. "Crying."

"What about him?" Matteo asked, nodding to Five.

"Don't touch him," Jane said with a commanding tone. "He's mine."

Kelly followed Jane into the stairwell. The decent of twenty-nine floors would not only be quicker than the elevator but easier.

"Wait."

She paused at the top of the first flight, barely masking her irritation. "What, Kelly? I don't have time to go into couples therapy right now to discuss our communication, intimacy, and respect issues.."

Her words were biting, but Jane watched as a smile tugged at the corners of Kelly's mouth. "That's not why I asked you to wait."

"Then spit it out. I'm working."

Kelly gripped the stair railing, his white knuckles tensing with each word. "Let me help. Whatever you need. I've got your six."

Jane let out a perturbed and not-so-confident sigh. "Fine. But lose the tuxedo, James Bond."

Kelly grinned. "I thought it was sexy. You don't?"

Jane did a double take and muttered one word under her breath before heading down the stairwell. "Maybe."

Refusing to ride in the police cruiser, Jane hailed one of the few remaining yellow cabs in New York City, barking out the address to Kelly's apartment.

"You remembered," he said with a grin.

"I remember everything."

"Of course, you do."

As the car sped down the West Side Highway, Jane leaned back, closing her eyes to catch her breath. Kelly seized the moment, gently taking her hand. His finger traced the small cut on the inside of her left wrist—the mark left from cutting Martin Pearl down from the noose.

"What now?" Kelly asked, not letting go of her hand.

"Now, you change clothes, and we score some…" Jane glanced at the cabbie, who seemed lost in his own world. "We score some *food*."

Kelly stared out the window, absently rubbing his bottom lip with his free hand, still keeping hold of Jane's. "I have a better idea. Hey," Kelly leaned into the cab's grimy partition. "Take us to Chinatown—corner of Canal and Elizabeth."

He sat back with a satisfied smirk.

"What are you doing?" she asked, her voice laced with skepticism.

"You said you needed *food*," Kelly said, nodding toward the cabbie. "I'm getting you *Chinese* food."

Jane paid for the cab in cash and joined Kelly on the street corner as their ride pulled away. Tugging at his bow tie, Kelly unbuttoned the top two buttons of his over-starched shirt. "C'mon," he said, taking Jane by the hand. "Let's do this."

"What the hell are *we* doing?"

Kelly turned to her as they climbed the stairs to the front door of the NYPD 5th Precinct. "I'm getting you food."

"What?"

He lowered his voice, talking out of the side of his mouth. "From the evidence locker."

Jane dropped Kelly's hand, backing down the stairs. "Too many cameras. I'll meet you down there," she said, pointing.

"Where?"

"Taste of Shanghai."

"Fine. But stay there."

"Don't tell me what to do."

Kelly shot her a scowl before disappearing into the Precinct. Once he was inside, Jane crossed the street, pausing on the corner to allow traffic to pass. With each step, she realized the restaurant was dark—missing closing time by fifteen minutes. Leaning against the side of the building, she propped one leg on the brick wall for support while watching the last two college kids exit. The bells over the door jingled as the store owner locked up, casting a dirty look her way. No doubt they thought she was there to buy drugs. And she was.

Jane rolled her eyes and moved down to wait for Kelly under the cover of a dark awning. The hair on the back of her neck prickled with unease, and she glanced down the alley beside her, casually scratching her back while gripping the gun tucked into her waistband.

She yawned just as two lowlifes skulked out of the alley. "Hey baby," said the tall one with a sneer.

Jane didn't engage.

"I said, *hey baby.*"

"*What?*" Jane snapped, her voice sharp with confident anger.

"Now, don't be like that."

Jane looked past the men, searching for Kelly. She could've scored some dope on her own by now and a lot closer to Central Park West. Jane needed to get rid of Five's body before sunrise. "Look guys, I don't want any trouble."

"Then hand over your bag, and no one gets hurt."

Jane responded to their threat with a perturbed sigh. "Boys, I can *guarantee* you don't want to do this."

The shorter one placed a hand on the brick wall behind Jane, leaning in close to her face. His hot, rancid breath hit her before his words. "Don't spit that shit at me, bitch. Give me the motherfuckin' bag, or I'll bleed you all over this street."

"*Really?*" Jane scoffed with a sarcastic laugh. "Go on. Keep walking."

"Fuck you."

"Last chance," Jane said, her voice eerily calm.

"What'd I just say, bitch?"

Without warning, Jane drove her knee into the tall one's balls, pulling her gun with lightning speed, cracking him on the head with the butt of her Glock. It was over before he knew it had begun.

His friend hesitated for a split second before deciding to stay and fight. Jane cocked her head and curled her fingers, beckoning him to her. "Let's go, boy. I'll give you a beat down you'll remember for the rest of your life. And tomorrow when everyone asks you what happened to your face, you can tell them you got your ass kicked by a girl," she said, stepping over his buddy's limp body.

He lunged at Jane, throwing a wild punch, but her quick parry deflected the kid's powerful yet clumsy blow. Without hesitation, she countered, landing a right hook to his unshaven face.

Blood exploded from his broken nose, spraying crimson streaks across the store window behind him as his head snapped to the side. Shaking off the punch, he spat a glob of blood onto the sidewalk before bending down to snatch a snub nose .38 Special from his buddy's pocket. His fingers trembled with rage as he aimed the cold steel between Jane's eyes.

"You wanna dance, bitch," he growled, wiping blood from his nose with the back of his hand, smearing it across his face like war paint. "Hand over the bag, or I'll shoot you in the face."

Jane's gun was already swinging at her side. "I've given you every chance, and you've blown them all. Why don't you walk away while you still can."

"Fuck you, bitch," he spat, cocking the gun and stepping closer.

In a flash, Jane shoved his hands skyward, gripping the pistol and ducking her head as he fired a shot into the air. The deafening blast echoed through the street, but Jane was already in motion, driving her knee into his junk with vicious force. He doubled over with a strangled grunt, the breath knocked from his lungs. Seizing the moment, Jane overpowered him, twisting his wrist and jamming the snub-nosed gun into his gut with enough force to crack a rib.

He staggered back, gasping, his eyes wide with pain and terror as Jane ripped the gun from his hands. Without hesitation, she aimed both weapons at this head, her grip steady—her eyes cold. With her finger hovering dangerously close to the trigger, she cocked her head, a wicked smile curling her lips.

"Surprise, motherfucker."

His voice trembled. "Don't shoot, lady! Don't shoot!" He clutched at his gut with one hand and his balls with the other.

Jane arched a brow, her voice maintaining the same cold, menacing tone. "You holding?"

His breath hitched. "You a cop?"

"*Fuck* no," Jane snapped. She repeated her question with biting clarity. "Do you have dope or not?"

The man grimaced, still clutching his side. Jane felt only the faintest flicker of remorse for what she'd done to him. "You don't look like no junkie, lady."

"Forget it," Jane said, her patience now razor-thin. "I'll find someone else."

He slumped against the brick wall, his bloody nose dripping onto his shirt. "You buyin'?"

Jane's eyes narrowed, her icy glare cutting through him. "Don't waste any more of my time."

The man leaned down to once again pick the pocket of his unconscious partner in crime. Jane stopped him. "Don't move, or you'll take your last breath."

His hands shot up in surrender. "It's in his pants," he stammered.

Jane nudged the unconscious man's pant pocket with her foot, her gun still trained on them. "Fine. Get it out."

The man hesitated, then pulled a tiny bag of heroin from his buddy's pocket, holding it between two trembling fingers. He handed it up to Jane like an offering. "Take it. Don't shoot me."

Jane kept her gun trained on him, tossing a fifty-dollar bill at his feet like a scrap to a starving animal. "Take it and get out of here. And don't try that shit with anyone else. Got it?"

Wincing in pain, he gave her a tight nod. Jane crossed the street, tucking the .38 Special into the pocket of her hoodie. As she rounded the corner, Kelly came bounding down the steps of the Precinct.

"I have bad news," he said, resting his hands on his hips in defeat. "There was nothing in the evidence room."

Jane spotted a cab and whistled, the sharp note piercing the night air. She threw up her hand, casting Kelly a brief, dismissive glance. "I need to go."

"Didn't you hear me?"

"I heard you," Jane mumbled as she slid into the backseat. "Just because you can't complete an assignment doesn't mean I'm equally incompetent."

She shut the door just as Kelly pounded the cab with his open palm. "Wait! I'm coming with you."

"You're slowing me down," she said through the window before barking at the driver. "Go."

As the cab sped off, Kelly's shout trailed behind. "Answer your damn phone, will ya!"

Jane raised a hand out the back window as a sign he'd been heard while a neighbor flung open their window and yelled, "Shut the fuck up down there!"

"Hey!" Kelly shot back. "Kiss my ass!"

"Prom's over, fucknut! Go home!"

DAY FOUR | 0800 HOURS

Jane sat in the corner booth of a diner at 72nd and Columbus Avenue. The breakfast crowd was picking up, which meant it was time for her to go. By the time she returned to the El Dorado, Tariq Maski—better known to Jane as Five—was already dead. Only then did she realize she was out of practice with dosing succinylcholine on the fly. There would be no interrogation, no chance for her to get answers before she finished him off. It was unfortunate, because while her dosing skills had gotten rusty, her speech—delivered to make him painfully aware he was dying at the hands of a woman— was still fresh as a daisy in her mind.

She packed his lifeless body into a black construction bag, moving quickly as she dragged it to the oversized trash chute near Martin Pearl's front door. She checked her surroundings for cameras or witnesses before dropping him in.

Collecting him at the bottom of the chute, Jane then tossed him into an abandoned vinyl basket truck with a bad wheel she found in the basement of the El Dorado.

Improvise. Adapt. Overcome.

Jane propped the body in the first alley she found, teeming with homeless men. Then, injecting half of the heroin into his system, she put the rest in his pocket. NYPD would report it as an overdose—Jane would make sure of it, even if she had to involve Kelly. Her bigger concern was who Five was working with.

Jane ran her fingers across the book and took a sip of her lukewarm coffee, her eyes lingering on the cover of *Charlotte's Web*. She was mentally replaying the events of the last four days when, without warning, a man slid into the booth across from her, uninvited.

Brown hair, late thirties, and in decent shape by Jane's estimation, he carried a coffee-stained diner mug and a well-worn satchel slung loosely over one shoulder. Tucked under his arm were a newspaper and a copy of *The Trumpet of the Swan* by E.B. White. As he settled into the booth, he placed the book title side up on the table, then locked eyes with Jane, blinking only once.

He was unremarkable, save for one glaring detail: the red scarf slung around his shoulders clinging to his weathered brown leather jacket like an unwelcome lover.

Jane was exhausted, sore, and in desperate need of sleep, but she was always vigilant and not one to believe in coincidence. He clearly knew who she was. But who the hell was he?

Jane remained perfectly still. She didn't speak, didn't flinch as her fingers discreetly brushed against the pearl handle of the knife tucked in the front pocket of her hoodie. Taking a life in a crowded diner, in broad daylight, wasn't on the agenda to-day—but if it came to that, she'd rise to the occasion. Already formulating an idea of how to kill him, she would slide in next to him and slip the blade between his ribs, puncturing his heart. Jane could eliminate him and be out of the diner before he took his last breath.

"Welcome home, Jane." He had a disturbing grin, like a politician who could smile and lie or a priest who could do the same.

Jane studied him carefully. His pale skin, brown hair, and eyes revealed little, but the spiral top of a reporter's notebook peeking from his satchel and the ink stain marring the middle finger of his right hand intrigued her. Jane had no idea who he was, but she was wary of what he wanted.

"Yeah," he continued, looking away and back to her. "I heard you were a tough nut to crack."

Jane remained silent.

"You were a busy girl last night."

Her heartbeat quickened, but she masked it with practiced ease, holding her breath to keep her emo-tions in check. With each deliberate blink of her heavy eyelids, Jane found her center, finally exhaling in a slow, dismissive sigh.

"It's fine. You don't have to say anything," the man said. "Just listen."

An aging waitress walked by, refilling Jane's empty coffee mug. "Doing okay over here?"

Jane nodded, her eyes fixed on the face of the man opposite her. As the waitress walked away, Jane took a slow sip of her coffee, her steely gaze unbro-ken. "You have one minute."

"My name is Levi Grant."

"And?"

"Hey, don't waste my minute with your own words."

He slid the folded newspaper across the table toward her. It was *The New York Times*—the daily crossword front and center. Nearly every square was filled in—in ink. Either Levi Grant was flaunting his brilliance, or he was sending her a message.

"I wanted to talk to you about a friend of mine—Matt Matthews. I understand he was a friend of yours as well."

The mention of Matt's name caught Jane off guard. She almost panicked—almost. Instead, Jane's eyes scanned each corner of the diner, looking once again for cameras. She'd cased the place before sitting down, but talking to Levi Grant and hearing Matt's name felt dangerous. And if there was one thing Jane trusted above all, it was her gut.

"There aren't any," Levi said.

"What?" Jane's eyes snapped back to his face.

He scribbled *CAMERAS* in bold blue ink across the top of the newspaper and turned the crossword toward her. "Muffins. They're out of blueberry muffins," he said, his finger tapping the word before casually moving on to five down.

He was masking his words. Intrigued, Jane leaned in, her eyes scanning the puzzle, eager to uncover what else Levi Grant might know. When she located five down, the word wasn't a thirteen-letter word for: *in a way that leaves no doubt.* Instead of *UNEQUIV-OCALLY*, the word *THUNDERSTRUCK* stared back at her.

Jane shot Levi an annoyed glance tempered by a casual shrug.

Unfazed, he pointed to the six-letter, two-word answer: *a small, rustic dwelling (Abbr.)*. Instead of *LOG CAB*, which Jane would have chosen, the answer was *RED FOX*.

Jane's gaze drifted to the red scarf coiled around Levi's neck, a spark of curiosity igniting within her. Without hesitation, she pulled the newspaper closer for inspection. Some of the answers were correct, but mingled among the letters were two names: *Maggie Thompson* and *Martin Pearl*—the senator killed in the MTA bombing and the very man Jane had saved less than twelve hours ago.

Without revealing her thoughts, she matched Levi's stare.

"I understand you're looking for a place in New York City," he said.

Jane didn't react.

Levi slid a business card across the table. Jane glanced at the real estate agent's card, which had a face, phone number, and name: *Frank Turner*.

"If you're ever in the market for an apartment in the city, I think you'll find a visit with this agent very … *eye-opening*."

Levi Grant gathered his things and slid out of the booth. Jane did the same, tucking the newspaper through a small opening of her backpack. "Hope you don't mind if I keep this," she said. "The real estate section and all."

"No problem."

He tossed some bills on the table, stuffing a noticeable wad of cash into the front pocket of his worn jeans. Jane led the way out of the diner, pausing on the street to adjust her backpack. When she turned around, he was gone, leaving only a glimpse of red in the distance.

Jane eyed the business card again, then focused her attention on the drugstore across the street. She would, in fact, give Mr. Turner a call, but first, she needed a second phone.

———

KELLY CASEY SAT on the edge of the bed in Christina Templeton's swanky Soho apartment. Still in his tuxedo, his black tie from the night before hung loosely in one hand, his head in the other. As he watched her sleep, he couldn't help but wonder how she'd react to his abrupt departure from the gala.

As he listened to Christina's shallow breathing, Kelly was fully aware that this fleeting silence would be the last moment of peace she'd offer him today. Kelly's stomach twisted with guilt—it was a dick move leaving her without saying goodbye, but what choice did he have? Jane wasn't answering her phone, and if he was going follow up on the lead the journalist gave him, he had to follow Matteo.

He didn't want to lie to Christina, but he didn't know how to tell her the truth.

"You're here." Her sleepy voice was soft and slightly hoarse, no doubt remnants of the night before.

"I'm here for *you*," Kelly replied. "Which is where I should've been last night. I'm sorry."

Christina sat up in bed, her bleary eyes and tousled hair making her seem innocent and sweet. Kelly knew better. Christina Templeton was quite possibly the original honey badger. Small and seemingly harmless, she was actually quite dangerous when pushed too far. Right now, Kelly had no idea how far he'd pushed her.

"I should be furious with you, Kelly," she said, a pout forming on her lipstick-stained mouth. "But I know duty calls. I only wish you would pick up the phone. I worry about you."

Off the bed and standing with his hands in his pockets, Kelly tried to hide his surprise. Never in a million years had he expected this response. Last night's gala was a culmination of a year's worth of work on Christina's part, and the fact that Kelly pulled an Irish exit was, by any standard, unacceptable. Yet, she wasn't angry.

"I respect you more than that, Christina," Kelly said, waiting to catch her eye. "I respect *myself* more than that. I'm sorry."

Christina slipped out of bed, her silk nightgown whispering against her skin as she moved. Standing behind Kelly, she wrapped her arms around him, pulling him into a tight embrace. She smelled of expensive facial cream and the lingering notes of her perfume. "Make love to me," she whispered, her voice a soft invitation as her hand slipped beneath his tuxedo shirt, her fingers tracing the lines of his chest.

Kelly gently wrestled her hands away from his body. He knew it was over, but he didn't want to hurt her. He was an unselfish man and lover—a giver— but he no longer had anything to give to Christina. In the time they'd spent together, he'd never told her he loved her— because he didn't. Now, his thoughts were consumed by his job and the people who'd died on his watch. And Jane—she occupied just as much space in his mind. He needed to talk to her about their relationship, about how it ended. Kelly was at a crossroads, and he knew it.

Christina kissed him on the cheek, her lips slowly moving toward his mouth. Kelly pulled away abruptly, taking both her hands in his. "I need to go home, take a shower, and get to the office."

She pulled away and stepped back. "What's going on?"

Kelly sighed, his shoulders dropping. "Listen," he began. After that one word, Christina turned around, walked into the bathroom, and closed the door behind her.

Moments later, he heard the shower running. He knocked before letting himself in. Standing naked under the water, Christina flashed him a seductive smile. He knew what she was trying to do, but it wasn't going to work.

"I can't do this anymore, Christina."

"Fine," she said, turning away. "Goodbye."

"We need to talk—" Kelly stopped himself. He didn't want things to end like this. "Okay. I'm gone."

Christina raised a hand in a silent farewell but didn't turn around.

As Kelly walked away from Christina's apartment, he pulled out his phone and Dailed Jane. Silently, he prayed for her to pick up the phone. When she didn't, Kelly did the only thing he could. He left a message.

"Look, I don't know where you are or where you're staying while you're in the city, but I'm still in the same apartment. You know where the key is. I'll handle the Martin Pearl situation, but I need to see you. Call me back."

DAY FOUR | 1100 HOURS

Jane stared at the number on the business card as she peeled the protective plastic from her new burner phone. With practiced ease, she inserted the SIM card, powered it up, and dialed.

"Hello, you've reached Frank Turner. I'm away from my phone, but leave your name and number, and I will return your call as soon as possible. If there's a specific property you'd like to see, leave the MLS information in your message. Thank you, and have a good day."

As the voicemail played, Jane flipped through the newspaper, landing on a property in Kips Bay. It was Kelly's neighborhood and the one she knew the best.

"Mr. Turner, my name is…ah, Charlotte Henry. I was interested in seeing a listing on East 30th Street. Apartment 4B? If you could call me back, I'd love to have a showing today."

Jane left the MLS and her new phone number before hanging up. Saving his contact as *Agent*, she slipped the phone into her pocket. After purchasing a

MetroCard with cash, Jane boarded the 2 train heading downtown.

As the subway car jolted with each stop, Jane wondered if he'd be home. She wondered if the key was still hidden in the same spot?

And she wondered what the hell she was doing.

After her briefing last night with Blackwood, Jane was more unsure of her assignment than ever. All her old boss seemed to know was that high-ranking officials in the U.S. government were being targeted. The plans underway by enemies of the state were vague, but if *Red Fox* could shed some light on what was about to go down, Jane wasn't above doing the recon.

When she stepped off the train near Kelly's apartment, Jane whispered a silent prayer he wouldn't be home. She wasn't sure if she was ready for the conversation that awaited them. Jane loved Kelly—if that was what love was. She trusted him, cared for him deeply, and genuinely enjoyed his company. But whenever thoughts of Matt Matthews crept into her mind—and they always did—Jane didn't hide what she felt.

It wasn't that she would, or even *could,* leave Kelly for Matt. But Kelly had once told her that he could never compete with a dead man. In death, Matt could do no wrong.

Jane was loyal. She carried a deep sense of responsibility to those who had sacrificed their lives to protect hers. Jennifer Drenkowski was the first—gunned down like an animal in Afghanistan when rebels mistook her for Jane. And Matt, who had taken a bullet to save her life.

If push came to shove, Jane had no doubt Kelly

would do the same. But the fact remained: he hadn't. Matt had. In Jane's mind, there was something to be said for that kind of devotion.

As Jane strolled past the playground in Kelly's apartment complex, she paused, watching the children giggling as they swung and climbed the slide. Young mothers played with their little ones, and Jane lingered, her thoughts drifting. When she lived with Kelly, this had been one of her favorite pastimes. Kelly once said it was because her own childhood was shortchanged, and that's why Jane found solace in the carefree laughter of the children in their building. Or maybe, Jane thought, it was simply their innocence that fascinated her—the endless possibilities awaiting a child who had the love and support of someone who cared.

Kelly thought her fascination with children was a sign she wanted her own—that her maternal instincts were kicking in. But Jane had been quick to counter, listing countless reasons why she shouldn't bring a child into a world so riddled with chaos and uncertainty. Kelly, however, pushed back, "That's exactly why people have children, Jane. It's the hope for a better world—a better life for their child. That's what children are—hope made real through love."

Jane didn't argue with him. Not because she agreed, but because she couldn't fully understand what he meant. Chaos was all she had ever known. From the moment she was born until the day she ended Three's life, her existence had been a relentless cycle of turmoil and survival. Chaos wasn't just her reality—it was the world she'd learned to navigate, the one where she'd found a way to thrive.

Leaving Coywolf and returning to civilian life

hadn't been easy for Jane. And while Kelly did his best to accommodate her needs, Jane struggled to accept the kind of love he wanted to give her. That was the heart of their struggle. In Jane's mind, if she'd never been taught how to love, how could she possibly love someone well?

Jane was smart, savvy, and—according to Kelly—beautiful, but even his love couldn't bridge the chasm of her emotional unavailability. The one psychiatrist Jane visited after their breakup, before her exit to Sweden, had explained that people who struggle to accept love often do so because they feel unworthy of it. Jane felt worthy of many things. Love, not so much.

It was something that haunted Jane in the quiet hours of the night. Had she truly felt so unlovable as a child that she would never allow herself to fully open up to anyone?

Standing outside Kelly's apartment building, a feeling of familiarity washed over her. Dinners, movies, baseball games … Kelly always wanted Jane to experience what he imagined as a normal life—*his* version of normal. And although some of it was enjoyable for Jane, it never felt *normal*.

Without a key card to swipe her way in, Jane lingered near the building's entrance, waiting for her opportunity. When a delivery person pushed through the door, she silently slipped in behind him, moving swiftly before it closed. Security cameras dotted every corner of Kelly's building, and although her face had once been familiar to them six years ago, she wasn't taking any chances. Jane pulled up her hoodie, kept her head down, and blended into the shadows.

As the elevator rose to the seventh floor, memories and anxieties she'd pushed aside were flooding her mind. Kelly wanted to understand her, and the harder he tried, and closer he got to Jane's true self, the more she pulled away. She was terrified of letting anyone in far enough to gain a hold on her. The thought of losing that kind of control—of being vulnerable and unable to walk away—sent a cold panic through her.

When she reached Kelly's apartment, she fumbled with the fire extinguisher cabinet next to his front door, standing on her tiptoes as her hand skimmed over the dust-covered metal top. A single key dropped into her waiting palm, and she smiled. There was something oddly comforting about knowing she could still get into his apartment—that she still had access to that place in her heart and mind where, for a time, she'd felt secure.

Jane turned the key in the lock and pushed through the door into the apartment without a sound. It was late enough in the morning that Kelly shouldn't be home, but she didn't want to risk drawing attention to herself. If living in this apartment with Kelly taught her anything, it was that the walls of his apartment were paper-thin.

As she placed the key into the familiar blue glass bowl by the door, Jane instantly realized she wasn't alone—Kelley's keys were already there. Moving cautiously through the apartment, the sound of running water drifted from the bathroom. She had two choices: leave now or stay and face the music.

While weighing her options, Jane couldn't help but notice how unfamiliar the apartment felt. Aside from his father's antique desk by the door and the bowl his mother had given him, nearly everything else had changed.

The once masculine home, filled with dark wood, athletic jerseys, and scattered, ragtag knickknacks, had been replaced by a sea of white and beige. The walls displayed carefully curated art, and the black and white photos seemed as if they'd been pulled from a catalog. The whole place looked less like a home, and more like a perfectly staged set—the kind influencers use to sell beauty products.

"Jesus, Kelly. I don't know who she is, but she's got you by Joanna Gaines' dick."

She moved closer to the bathroom, straining to listen. If Kelly's girlfriend was in the shower with him, she'd definitely need to make a quick exit. But all she heard was the steady sound of falling water and the occasional cough. He was alone. Kelly wasn't one to stay silent in the presence of a naked woman.

Jane wandered into the kitchen, opened the refrigerator, and stared in shock at the neatly lined rows of water and green juice. "Who *are* you?" she whispered, nabbing a bottle of water. Making herself comfortable on the deep sectional couch, she settled in to wait.

By the time she'd cracked the cap and downed half the bottle, Kelly was out of the shower, walking around the apartment naked while toweling off his red hair. He looked as good as ever, and Jane averted her gaze, not wanting to appear too eager when he finally caught her eye.

Kelly strolled into the kitchen, removing a green juice from the fridge. The moment he spotted Jane, he jumped, instinctively reaching for a loaded gun on the kitchen counter. "What the shit!"

Without flinching, Jane's lips curled into a tiny smile. "What the shit?"

"Damnit, Jane," Kelly muttered, lowering the gun to his side. He made no moves to cover himself, and Jane enjoyed the view.

"What are you—did you get my message?" he asked.

Jane shook her head.

"I called you—*again.* I wanted to make sure you knew I was still living here, and the key was in the same spot. But I guess, as usual, you didn't need my help."

"I still need your help."

Kelly cocked his head to one side, placing his hands on his bare hips. "Really?" His tone carried a hint of disbelief.

"I need you to convince all the right people that Martin Pearl is dead."

A shadow of disappointment crossed Kelly's face before he looked away, still not bothering to cover up.

"Are you purposely standing there naked?"

He smirked, frustration still etched on his face. "Nothing you haven't seen before."

"True."

"If you didn't get my message, then why are you here?"

Jane shrugged. "I'd love to say I like what you've done with the place, but this doesn't look like…"

"Like what?" Kelly asked, stepping closer, casually draping the white towel around his neck instead of his waist.

"*You.*"

Kelly gripped the towel with both hands and

glanced around the apartment before popping his ginger brows. "Maybe I'm not the same person you knew six years ago."

Jane's eyes scanned him from head to toe, her face unreadable. "You *look* like the same person."

"I'll take that as a compliment."

"Seriously, though, what's with all the white?" She asked, motioning to the apartment.

Kelly shrugged, taking a step closer to Jane. "I hired a decorator. Believe it or not, after getting dumped and left heartbroken, I thought changing my surroundings might make me feel like I'd moved on."

"How'd that work out for you?"

Kelly bit the corner of his bottom lip but didn't answer. "I'd really like to talk to you, Jane. God knows I would. But I have a fake suicide to write up, a grieving family to lie to, and then, somehow, console."

"It's for their own good," Jane said, looking away.

"I'll try to weave that into my discussions with them. Now," Kelly said, taking another step in Jane's direction. "You still haven't told me why you're really here."

Jane cast her eyes to the floor as his naked body inched closer. "I have a meeting today in this part of town, and I needed a place to crash … and maybe shower."

Kelly finally wrapped the towel around his waist and sat across from Jane in an oversized chair. With his legs spread wide, she could still see everything about Kelly Casey that had once been hers. "Tell me what's going on—the ten-thousand-foot version."

"I'm confused," Jane said.

"You don't get to say that. That's my line. Now tell me where you've been hiding out for the past few years and why you're back in New York—because I know it's not for me."

Jane saw the hurt in Kelly's eyes, and in that moment, she felt like a selfish, arrogant bitch. Aside from Matt, Kelly was the only man who'd ever loved her completely—for who she was. It wasn't until she saw him again that she realized how much she'd compartmentalized and shoved aside while living in Stockholm.

She came clean, spilling everything in one breath. "I've been in Stockholm." Jane paused, watching Kelly's face for a reaction. "Sweden," she added. "I have a place there."

"All this time you've been in Stockholm?"

"I've been going to school. In the past six years, I've earned a bachelor's degree in engineering and a master's in software engineering. I was one day away from defending my PhD thesis when an assassin was sent to kill me."

Genuine concern flashed across Kelly's face. "Who would want to—"

"Coywolf," Jane said, interrupting. "They came for me, but not for the reasons I expected. It was a test. I took out their assassin, grabbed my go-bag, and left. I contacted Dr. Hudson, defended my thesis the next morning, and hopped on a train to Oslo. Peter got me from there to D.C."

"What do they want from you?"

Jane shrugged. "There are some powerful, well-connected people plotting to assassinate high-ranking officials in the U.S."

Kelly's eyes widened. "What are you talking about?"

"Exactly what I said, Kelly. Your MTA bombing wasn't about mass casualties—though I'm sure they celebrated that. I believe the real target was Congresswoman Maggie Thompson."

Kelly's face paled, and he dropped his head in his hands to fist his hair in frustration. "*Shit*. This all happened on my watch. I should've known—should've *seen* something."

"How?" Jane asked. "I had the absolute best backdoor, underground information out there when I worked for Coywolf, and even *they* were blindsided. I think that's why they brought me back. Well," Jane looked away. "At least, that's what I was told."

Kelly knitted his brow. "What do you mean?"

"I think like a terrorist. Takes one to know one, I guess. Or something like that." Jane sighed, her eyes meeting Kelly's kind, familiar stare. For a moment, she wondered if he'd heard a word she said.

"It's taking every ounce of strength I have not to come over there and…"

"And what?"

"Hold you. Kiss you. Undress you right here and make love to you."

The truth was, Jane would've welcomed his kiss, but today wasn't the day to start something she wasn't sure she could finish. "I didn't come here to make you late for work. I just … I really need a shower while I wait for a phone call. So go to work, Kelly. I'll lock up on my way out."

Jane stood, and Kelly joined her. "You're coming back tonight."

She glanced around the apartment. "Seems like

maybe someone else might already be a regular here."

Kelly took a deep breath and walked toward his bedroom. "Yeah, maybe. You know where the towels are. Get a shower." He paused at the door, speaking over his shoulder. "You still have clothes in the guest room closet. They're in a garment bag."

"Really?"

Kelly shrugged, not turning to face her. "Sorry if they're wrinkled, but I didn't want …It would've seemed…*odd* if I kept an ex-girlfriend's clothes. You know, to other—"

"*Women*?" Jane put Kelly out of his misery. "Thanks. I didn't expect you to keep anything. I mean, I'm glad under current circumstances, but I would've understood if you'd …you know, burned them."

Kelly dropped his head to his chest, his voice soft and heavy with emotion. "No, baby. I held on to whatever was left of you."

Jane's stomach knotted. *Baby*—it was like a dagger to the heart. Kelly knew how she felt about him calling her that. He only used it when he wanted to show her how deeply he loved her.

Without another word, Kelly closed his bedroom door, and Jane made her way to the bathroom. The air was still heavy with steam and the familiar scent of Kelly's shower gel. "At least some things haven't changed," she said to herself.

Stepping into the shower, Jane carried with her every ounce of self-loathing she'd accumulated since the day she'd left.

AFTER RINSING off the grime and assigned kill of Tariq Maski, Jane stayed under the water until she heard the front door of the apartment close. Only then did she let out a deep sigh of relief. She was impressed with how well she'd compartmentalized her complicated history with Kelly to get into the mindset she needed for the job.

Stepping out of the shower, Jane padded to the one room that seemed to have escaped the decorator's touch—the guest room. She was anxious to dig through the clothes she'd left behind. When she threw open the double closet doors, she half-expected to find the garment bag buried behind forgotten Christmas decorations, but her clothes were front and center.

At the bottom of the closet, resting on top of a box, was a pair of her old running shoes, with her dirty socks still stuffed inside from the last time she wore them. A mix of surprise and emotion welled up inside her. Of all the things to keep, Kelly had held on to her worn-out shoes and dirty socks. The thought tugged at her heart—he hadn't just kept her things; he'd preserved pieces of her life, no matter how small.

Curious, Jane opened the box beneath the shoes. Inside, she found every card Kelly had ever given her in the year they were together. Each one ended with the same line: *I will love you forever, baby. XO K.*

Jane sank to the floor, sifting through the cards, searching for one particular memory—the one image of herself she had allowed him to keep. Jane didn't take photos, and she never allowed video. But she'd made an exception for Kelly—a single sketch drawn by a street artist on a cold autumn night in the West Village.

It had been one of their many dates. That night, they ate Indian food and listened to an unknown band. Jane hadn't brought a sweater or a coat, and Kelly—ever the gentleman—had taken off the sweater he wore over his shirt, draping it around her shoulders. As she snuggled into the collar, breathing in the essence of her man, a street artist approached them, asking if he could sketch them.

When Kelly requested that the sketch be of only Jane, the artist nodded and grinned, saying, "Yeah, man. I got you."

The artist asked Jane to pull Kelly's sweater up to her nose again, partially hiding her face. The result was an intimate portrait that captured Jane's essence without fully revealing her face.

Kelly loved that sketch, and Jane loved that he treasured it so. But when it wasn't in the box with what seemed to be everything Jane had left behind, she was surprised by how much it hurt. Seeing Kelly again had stirred emotions she'd buried over the last six years—feelings she wasn't quite ready to unpack.

When a phone rang out, Jane wasn't sure which of her two burners was getting a call. Seeing the blocked number, Jane assumed it was Silas Prince. She hoped he had some decent intel for her.

"Yeah," Jane answered.

"Seriously? *That's* how you answer your phone?" Silas asked, sounding mildly annoyed.

"Why do you care? More importantly, why are you calling?"

"Aren't you coming back to Maxtronix?"

"Not for a while. Why?"

"No reason. You left in a hurry and in that old BMW. Dr. Hudson wasn't thrilled about it."

"I don't work for Peter. Now, why did you call?"

"The Speaker of the House is dead. Did you hear? First, that Congresswoman and now the Speaker. If you ask me, something's definitely up."

The fact that Silas didn't know Martin Pearl was still alive gave Jane pause. What had Matteo told Peter about last night? And if they trusted Silas with Maxtronix secrets, why keep other kinds of information from him? Jane played along. "Yeah, I saw it on the news."

"And?" Silas pressed.

"And what?" Jane asked, now sifting through the row of perfectly pressed shirts and pants, each wrapped in plastic from the dry cleaners.

"That can't be a coincidence. I mean, the odds of both of them dying in the same week have to be a million-to-one."

"I don't know, Silas," Jane replied, distracted as she pulled the plastic off a pair of dark jeans and a red sweater—the outfit she wore on her first date with Kelly. She laid them on the bed and stepped back to admire them.

"Are you even listening to me, Jane?" He asked, his voice rising in frustration.

"Look, I hear you," she said, turning her attention back to the conversation. "But aren't you the mathematical genius from MIT?"

"Yes," he replied, full of confidence.

"Then why are you asking me about the odds? Something probably *is* going on, but what does it have to do with us?"

"I don't know how much you know about the

dark web, but there's a lot of chatter out there about the United States."

"Chatter?" The word caught Jane's attention. "Like what?"

"Like there's a coup in the works."

Jane paused. "What kind of coup?"

"Never mind," Silas muttered, his bravado faltering. "I'm probably just talking out of my ass."

Jane thought it but didn't say it. "Why did you call?"

"I'm supposed to send you some Maxtronix tech, but I don't know where to ship it. I thought you'd be back at the Potomac house by now."

"Maybe," Jane said, half-listening as her mind wandered. "I don't know when I'll be back. If I left anything behind, just throw it in the closet, okay?"

"I'm talking to you, Jane. Pay attention," Silas snapped before muttering under his breath, "*Kose Khahar.*"

Jane froze. She recalled Peter mentioning Silas spoke several languages. "I don't know who you think you are, but if you ever speak to me in that tone of voice—or call me a whore ever again—I will make sure you regret it. You got me?"

The silence on the line made Jane consider ending the call, but Silas piped up at the last second. "You'll have to excuse me. I sometimes forget myself. It's just that I know everything about you, Jane, and you know virtually nothing about me. If we're going to work together, I want there to be some respect between us."

"First off, Silas," Jane said, her voice lowering with each word, "you *don't* know everything about me—like the fact that I, too, speak Farsi. And second, where I come from, respect is something you earn. Think about that for a while and call me *only* when you have something important to say. Got it?"

Silas hesitated, then cleared his throat. "Where do you want me to send the SB?"

"What the hell is an SB?"

"Slaughterbot."

"Excuse me?" Jane asked, now hyper-focused on every word coming from Silas's mouth.

"It's a little something I've been working on at Max HQ. Dr. Hudson wanted you to have one in your tactical gear—whatever that means."

Jane was already fuming from the kid's attitude. She needed to hang up before she said something she'd regret—like threatening to hunt him down, tie him up, and cut off his balls with a rusty butter knife. "I'll get the Slaughterbot when I come back to Maxtronix, okay?"

As her second phone started ringing, Jane nearly hung up on Silas. "I gotta go."

"Wait—you have another burner phone?" He asked, his tone shifting.

"Goodbye, Silas."

Jane hurried to her backpack, fishing out the new phone. "Hello."

"Is this Charlotte Henry?"

"Yes."

"This is Frank Turner. You wanted to see the Kips Bay property on East 30th?"

"Yes," Jane replied, injecting as much enthusiasm into her voice as she could muster.

"The unit that you requested was just sold, but I've got another listing in the building next door. It's a bit bigger than what you were looking for and slightly more expensive, but—"

"Sure," Jane said, cutting in smoothly. "Bigger is better than smaller, right?"

"I'm just a few blocks away if you'd like to meet me there. I can text you the address and apartment number."

"Perfect. Give me thirty minutes?" Jane asked, running her fingers through her wet hair. She wasn't one to fuss over appearances, but a good impression was essential, and she needed to put on the dog.

"See you then, and Miss Henry?"

"Yes?"

"How did you get my name?"

Jane froze. It was a question she hadn't anticipated—figuring real estate agents didn't care where a client came from as long as they showed up. "Someone mentioned your name at the ah…" Jane fumbled her words, lightly tapping her forehead with her fist, trying to conjure a story. Her eyes landed on the coffee table in Kelly's living room, where an invitation lay among the magazines and remotes. "At the gala last night at the Pierre Hotel. I can't remember his name—we met so briefly."

Jane squeezed her eyes shut, praying the lie would stick.

"Alright. I'll see you soon."

Relieved, Jane hung up the phone and rushed to the bathroom, thinking maybe Kelly's current girlfriend had left behind a hairdryer or some makeup. It didn't seem like she lived with him, but Jane figured there had to be at least a drawer somewhere. She hoped it had a bra and some underwear that would fit.

DAY FOUR | 1400 HOURS

Kelly Casey sat across from the Secret Service agents and Speaker Pearl's wife, the weight of the past ninety minutes pressing down on him. He'd played his part—explaining, comforting, and ultimately convincing Mrs. Pearl that her husband was gone. The entire charade felt like walking on a razor's edge, with every word carefully chosen, every glance under scrutiny. His only solace was the presence of Mary Charles "Charlie" Madewell.

Charlie had been more than just a friend. She had patched him up after his messy breakup with Jane, even if their one-night stand had complicated things. Still, her presence grounded him. But today, Charlie was all business, her usual banter replaced by a cold professionalism. Speaker Pearl wasn't technically her responsibility, but as a high-ranking USSS officer, she was there to smooth things over, particularly for Li Hua Pearl, Martin's wife of forty years.

Finally, the room emptied. Mrs. Pearl, emotionally drained and convinced not to view her husband's body, was escorted out. The Kleenex box was bare, and the last of the staff disappeared behind closed doors. The performance was over—or so it seemed.

Kelly knew better. The real interrogation hadn't even started.

As soon as the door closed, Charlie's glare was laser-focused on him. They walked in silence down the hallway of One Police Plaza, the echo of their footsteps the only sound. Kelly knew he was about to get interrogated like a prisoner of war. Charlie never missed anything.

When they reached the exit to the parking lot, Charlie took his hand, her grip firm as she led him toward a black sedan parked in the shadows. "Get in," she ordered, her tone leaving no room for argument.

Kelly sighed—a deep exhale that signaled defeat, not just exhaustion. He slid into the backseat, knowing full well what awaited him. Charlie wasn't the type to let things slide, and right now, she had a look that said *no bullshit*.

The door clicked shut. In an instant, Charlie turned to face him, her expression stern. "What the hell is going on, Casey. And don't give me any of that scripted shit. You know I can read you like a damn book. Out with it."

Kelly dropped his head, squeezing his eyes shut. He wanted to tell her everything—about Speaker Pearl, about Jane crashing back into his life like a storm. But he couldn't. Not now. As much as he trusted Charlie—and he would stake his life on her— he couldn't afford to let anyone in at the moment. Too many moving pieces. Too much at stake.

He exhaled again, slower this time, and stuck to

the rehearsed line. "I don't know what you want me to say, Charlie."

"The fucking truth, Casey. That's what," Charlie snapped, her eyes narrowing. "Maybe Martin Pearl's wife bought that dog-and-pony show you pulled in there, but she's the only one. Now, where the hell is Martin Pearl's body? Did you lose it? Misplace it somewhere?"

She leaned in closer, her voice dropping to a deadly calm. "And don't think for a second that President Shaw won't be all over this. She, like me, can smell bullshit from five miles away. So, you can tell me what's going on now, or you can do it in front of a congressional committee—live on cable news. Your call. What's it gonna be?"

Charlie's words hit him like a punch to the gut. He dropped his head backwards to rest on the car seat and let out a low, pained groan.

"It can't be *that* bad, Casey," Charlie pressed, her tone softening just a fraction. "A man is dead, and for some reason, his Secret Service detail was none the wiser. Believe me, we've got our *own* bullshit to deal with, but right now, this is just you and me. Tell me the truth."

Kelly pushed the car door open and stepped out. Charlie followed, her nostrils flaring with each frustrated breath she took. Before she could utter her next *what the fuck*, Kelly reached for her hand, his voice low and measured. "Walk with me."

They strode in silence through the streets of Lower Manhattan while Kelly quietly shared what he believed he could safely divulge without putting Charlie—or anyone else—in danger.

"Let me get this straight." Charlie stopped midstride, her voice filled with disbelief. "You're telling me the reason you're acting so hinky is because Jane is back? Where has she been all this time?"

Kelly wanted to tell her that Speaker Pearl was alive, and Jane killed his would-be assassin, and that Matteo Caruso was more than Peter's partner—he was more than Kelly had ever envisioned.

"Tell me you're not lying, Kelly," Charlie said, her voice sharp with concern. "You're going to let this woman crawl so deep inside your head that it starts affecting your work? You realize the mess you're in, don't you?"

Kelly clenched his jaw. "You think I don't know how bad this is? For God's sake, Charlie, I'm already drowning in guilt. Senator Maggie Thompson, twelve others dead and dozens left injured—I'm carrying all of it."

"This is a mess from every angle," Charlie said under her breath.

Kelly nodded, shoving his hands deep into the pockets of his suit pants. "I get it, Charlie. From the outside, it looks like she's nothing but trouble. But Jane … she's not just some wildcard. She's exceptional. And trust me, she's valuable to a lot more people than just me."

Charlie scoffed at his words. "Valuable to who, Kelly? Because right now, I'm not seeing it."

"Kelly held her stare, fully aware Charlie knew he was leaving more unsaid than said. "You don't have to see it. But know she's not someone we can afford to underestimate."

"Why on earth would I underestimate the woman who wreaks havoc everywhere she goes?" Charlie took a step closer. "Besides, you know you still owe me for that mess years ago. I helped you clean up the deaths of terrorists and war profiteers—all against my better judgment."

Kelly tilted his head in reluctant agreement.

"You're such an asshole. You know that, right?"

"I know," Kelly replied, dropping his voice in defeat. "We should get back. The last thing I need is for people to see us together and start jumping to conclusions."

Charlie flirt-punched Kelly in the arm. "You know I don't like dick."

"I can think of one night you liked it."

"And one was enough."

"You know when you say things like that," Kelly said, lowering his head, "it makes me feel like not only did I fail to convince the woman I love to stay with me, but my best friend became a lesbian after sleeping with me."

"Yo, gingernuts," she said. "it's not like I blame you. You just helped me figure out who I really am. I love you for it. Take it as a compliment."

"Well, I'm sorry, but me, my dick, and my self-esteem don't feel that way."

As Kelly steered Charlie back toward police headquarters, she took him by the arm. "I *am* worried about you."

"Maybe worry about explaining to President Shaw how the Speaker of the House's secret service detail is missing."

"That's above my pay grade. Besides, you're the one who's got some explaining to do—and not just to me. I'm fairly certain there's a beautiful and exceptionally clingy woman you need to attend to. You know, the one who calls herself your girlfriend. And did I mention her father's a powerful senator?"

Kelly bobbled his head in agreement. Charlie wasn't just stating the facts—she was reminding him of the stakes.

"Call me when you figure out…whatever *this* is," Charlie said. "I'll help you. I've done it before."

It was true. Not only did she help him clean up the mess on the Potomac, Charlie was his shoulder to cry on when Jane left him in the middle of the night.

"It's what friends are for."

"You're more than my friend, Mary Charles," Kelly said, kissing her on the cheek. "You're my family."

"Yeah, fuck you too, Casey."

As they said their goodbyes, Kelly's phone lit up with Christina's name on the screen.

"Better take that one," Charlie said before mouthing the words *call me.*

"Hi," Kelly said, answering with as much enthusiasm as he could muster.

"Everything okay?" Christina's voice was soft, but the question hit Kelly like a hammer over the head.

He closed his eyes, trying to compose himself. Everything was obviously far from okay, yet she asked the question. Kelly felt a sudden, undeniable urge to end things—to tell her it was over. Kelly wanted to say to her that he would gather her things and send them by courier. That whatever he'd left at her place, she was free to throw out. Kelly wanted to be honest. He couldn't go on pretending their relationship was something it wasn't.

Instead, he said the universal code word that meant, *I'm not okay, but I'll pretend I am:* "Fine."

"You don't sound fine," Christina said, her voice a mix of concern and irritation.

Kelly picked up the pace, heading straight for his office. "I'm sorry I don't sound fine, Christina," he said, shutting the door with force. "I'm running on fumes. What did you need?"

"You don't have to be ugly about it, Kelly." She paused, her frustration starting to surface. "I'm calling about dinner. I could pick up something from Zabar's and bring it to your place. I'll cook and rub your back—or, *you know*, rub anything else you want."

Kelly wiped his tired eyes with the back of his hand and sighed, feeling the weight of the circumstances of his own making. "Not tonight, Christina. I'm working late. I don't know when I'll make it home."

Silence lingered on the line for a beat too long. "It's her, isn't it?" Christina said with measured certainty.

"*Who*?" Kelly did his best to act confused.

"It's written all over you. I know you better than you think."

He stopped dead in his tracks. This was it. It was time to tell the woman who loved him about the woman he loved.

"You're all bent out of shape about *her*," Christina said with confidence. "I figured you saw the news today, but I didn't know it would hit you this hard."

Kelly fumbled for the TV remote, his mind racing to catch up. "Who—who are we talking about?"

"Congresswoman Thompson," Christina said. "Her funeral is tomorrow. Daddy's going to Washington, D.C., for the whole ceremony. You need to stop beating yourself up, Kelly. You had nothing to do with her death or the others."

Kelly's jaw tightened, his anger striking like lightning in a storm. *How dare she.* How dare she try to tell him how to feel and what he was or wasn't responsible for.

"Christina, I can't—I'm *not* having this conversation with you. In fact, I think we need to take a break."

He was rational and business-like. And he was done. Breaking up over the phone wasn't necessarily the right thing to do. But here he was, doing it anyway.

The silence in response to his suggestion was thick and suffocating. He could hear Christina's shallow breaths, and in his mind, he pictured her breaking down in tears. When she didn't respond, he called out to her.

"Christina? Are you still there?"

"Yes, Kelly," she said, her voice strained with raw emotion. "I'm right where I've always been—at your beck and fucking call."

Kelly recoiled at the venom in her words. "Now, just a minute."

"No!" Christina's voice was sharp and trembling with indignation. "I cannot believe after all the days and nights I put up with your anger issues and your job—as a *cop*, no less. *Me* always putting *you* first, while you only cared about yourself."

Kelly's chest tightened, but his words shot back reflexively, "You're right. I don't deserve you. You deserve someone who can love you the way you need to be loved—not some two-bit cop from Pittsburgh. You've always been too for me, Christina. And I've known it all along."

"Don't you dare try that blue-collar bullshit with me, Kelly," she said, her voice now raw and furious. "I've heard you use that line before when you're trying to manipulate people—trying to make them feel safe like you're some misunderstood saint. I'm not a suspect you're trying to win over before interrogation. I'm your fucking girlfriend. And I deserve better than this."

Kelly squeezed the bridge of his nose, hoping to ease the rising ache in his head. "You do deserve better, Christina. You *are* better."

"So, am I still your girlfriend?" Her voice softened, a thread of hope woven into her anger. "Or did we just break up?"

Kelly inhaled, the words catching in his throat. "I can't do this anymore, Christina. You deserve more, and I'm not—" He hesitated, feeling the significance of the moment weighing down his words. "I'm not the man who can give it to you."

She allowed the silence to linger, her breath shallow on the other end. "So that's it. You're just going to flush a year of our relationship down the toilet in one phone call?"

"It was nine months," Kelly said, bringing his voice down.

"*What*?" She screeched.

"It's over, Christina"

"It's *over*?" she repeated as if daring him to take it back.

"Yes," Kelly said, his voice colder than he intended. "We need to sit down and talk about this face-to-face, but for now, I'll have anything you've left at my place boxed up and sent to you."

"You're packing up my stuff?" Her voice trembled with anger. "*You. You're* packing up my things and sending it back to *me. You're* breaking up with *me*?"

"Christina, don't make this any harder than it needs to be."

"She laughed bitterly, the sound ringing in his ears. "Fuck you, Kelly. This is about *her,* and you know it. You've kept her shit hanging in that closet for years like she might walk back through the door any second. And me? The woman who's stood by you, put up with your bullshit, and loved you through all of it? You're packing *my* stuff up."

Kelly swallowed hard. She knew. She'd always known, but hearing it spoken aloud was like a slap in the face. Christina saw through him, and somehow, that made him respect her for it. But it wasn't enough. She wasn't enough.

Because she wasn't Jane.

"Look," Kelly said, taking a deep breath, willing the words to come. "I'm sorry. For *everything*."

"I'm sorry too, Kelly," she spat. I'm sorry you're a fucking coward. I'm sorry I wasted my precious time on you. And if you think I'm packing up your shit and sending it back, you've got another thing coming!"

The line went dead. Kelly lowered the phone and sank into his desk chair, exhaling with a sigh of relief. It wasn't how he'd pictured it happening, but it was over. The calm he felt being out of the relationship was fleeting, replaced by a far heavier and more dangerous burden: the wrath of Senator Arthur Templeton.

Christina's father wasn't just powerful—he was relentless. With the ruthlessness of a mob boss, he destroyed careers, ruined reputations, and was rumored to have eliminated people when he needed to. He was the kind of man you wanted as an ally, not as an enemy. Arthur Templeton didn't just settle scores; he ruined lives.

Kelly rubbed his temples. "Well, shit. I've stepped in it now."

DAY FOUR | 1430 HOURS

Jane paced in front of the building, impatient, the same questions running through her mind on a loop: Why was she here? Who was Levi Grant, and what did he really know?

"Miss Henry?"

The voice came from behind her, and Jane froze —her instincts on high alert. She turned to face Frank Turner. He wasn't alone.

"Miss Henry?" He repeated.

Jane held her smile in place like a Southern woman determined not to show her displeasure. Inside, shock rippled through her like a cold current. She discreetly inhaled, drawing air deep into her lungs through her nose, and exhaled it with controlled disbelief through her parted lips. "Yes?"

"I'm Frank Turner. This is my associate, Mr. Farouk."

Jane's stare darted between the two men, keeping her eye contact to a minimum. She didn't need to look long to know who they really were. The recognition came flooding back as if not a single day had passed. The faces, the names, the unspeakable acts—

the atrocities she'd cataloged over the years—were now standing right in front of her, staring her squarely in the eye.

Jane had been back on United States soil for barely forty-eight hours, and yet here they were, out in the open as if hiding in the shadows was no longer necessary. That told her two things: the extremists she'd hunted for years had grown bold—brazen enough to step into the light and operate freely in America. And there was a plan to cause pain. Something was coming, something dark and devastating. Jane didn't know what it was yet, but she would— one way or another.

"No problem," she said, her smile fixed and un- wavering. "Thank you for fitting me in."

They entered the building, and Jane removed her sunglasses, taking a better look at the men. As they stepped into the elevator and the doors closed, Jane's mind raced. She mentally ticked off the crimes com- mitted by Faisal Tamimi, now posing as Frank Turner —his new American identity, a feeble attempt to hide the horrors of his past. Tamimi, a.k.a. Number Ten, was responsible for the bombing of a crowded Pak- istani market nearly nine years ago. Twenty-five people died that day, and countless others were in- jured. But Jane and Ten shared a far more personal connection.

Jane balled her fists, her fingers itching to reach for the knife hidden in her boot. She wanted nothing more than to drive the blade into Tamimi's throat—to feel the puncture of his flesh before watching the life drain from his eyes. His associate wouldn't fare any better—one discreet stab between the ribs would pop his heart like a water balloon, leaving both men to bleed out on the pristine elevator floor, staining its sleek surface with their betrayal.

But she couldn't. Not here. Not now.

She glanced above at the surveillance camera—its unblinking eye watching their every move. She wasn't dressed for covert ops. Instead, she wore the clothes of a woman in the market for a million-dollar apartment, carefully designed to fit the part.

She remembered the infrared bobby pin hidden in her hair. If it worked as promised, it would disrupt the camera feed. But that wasn't what concerned her at the moment.

Jane worried Tamimi might recognize her.

They'd met before. Afghanistan. Years ago. She'd been a ghost then, moving through the shadows and eliminating high-profile targets with her unit. Tamimi, along with Number Three, had put a hefty bounty on her head after she took out two of Three's top men in a single day—sniping them from a ridge without so much as a flinch. The reward they placed was steep—enough to entice the worst of the worst.

But it wasn't Jane who paid the price. It was her best friend.

Fellow Marine Jennifer Drenkowski had been mistaken for Jane and captured in her place. Jane could still see the footage—the memory burned into her mind like a scar that would never heal. She'd watched every single second of that videotape: the brutal rape, the savage beheading, even the dismemberment of her body—all while the animals they called soldiers laughed. And in the center of the horror stood Tamimi—cackling with delight, participating in the rape and desecration of Jennifer.

Now, he was standing right in front of her.

"It's a lovely building," Tamimi said, his voice laced with false charm. "And the neighborhood is excellent for families. PS 116 is just down the street." He paused, his eyes narrowing. "Do you have children?"

"No." Her voice was calm, though every fiber of her being screamed to gut him right on the spot. "At least none that I know about, right?" she said, finding her footing.

It was a jab at the practice of Sharia Law, where procreation was encouraged, but any child born outside of a legitimate marriage would be classified as Walad az-Zina, a child of sin.

Jane's comment was bold and deliberate—a direct challenge of everything Tamimi and his associate believed. She saw it in their reactions: the flicker of disapproval in their eyes, the tightening of their jaws. It was subtle but unmistakable. These men followed a strict code, and her remark was unacceptable.

The only reason there were two of them meeting Jane was because it would've been inappropriate—improper, by their standards—for either of them to be alone with a woman. That was the kind of control they operated under, one where women were devalued.

Women under their rule were second-class citizens. Girls weren't allowed to go to school after the age of ten. And hatred for the Western world was deeply rooted in nearly everything they did.

No. Tamimi would never be alone with Jane in public. But alone with *him* was exactly what Jane wanted—ten minutes. Alone. Maybe less.

He shot her a dirty look but held his tongue. Jane guessed that securing the sale—or at least the illusion of it—was more important to him than voicing his disdain. When Tamimi opened the door to the apartment, Jane was legitimately impressed. The home had been beautifully staged and was, quite frankly, filled with impressive "wow" factors.

Jane wandered from room to room, seizing every moment out of direct sight to arm herself. She discreetly slid an extra knife into her boot and shoved her loaded Glock deeper into the waistband of her jeans, pressing against the expensive lace panties she'd borrowed from the one drawer Kelly allowed his girlfriend.

"The appliances are new," Tamimi said, prattling on as he walked the floor plan. "The washer and dryer are also included."

"It's stunning," Jane replied, moving through the kitchen. She paused at the entrance of one of two bathrooms in the apartment, turning on the light to catch a glimpse of herself in the mirror. "Do you mind if I use the restroom?"

The two men exchanged glances before looking back at her.

"If it's inconvenient, I can wait," she added. "It's just I drank a cup of coffee while I was waiting to meet with you and—"

"Be my guest," Tamimi interrupted, waving her off. The look on his face made it clear he had no interest in hearing about her bodily functions.

Inside the bathroom, Jane placed her backpack on the vanity and swiftly dug to the bottom. Sealed in a plastic bag were several VitalWatch patches left over from her presentation in Stockholm. Invisible to the human eye, the VitalWatch was incredibly accurate, recording and transmitting from anywhere in the world to a program that saved every word, sound, and image while GPS recorded their location in real time.

Jane flushed the toilet and ran the faucet briefly before carefully peeling one of the VitalWatch patches from its static-free backing. Attaching it to the tip of her right index fingernail, Jane took a deep breath. She had to execute the placement flawlessly.

Out of the bathroom, Jane bided her time, waiting for the perfect moment. She needed to somehow touch Tamimi's neck just below the ear—the optimal location for the device to capture everything. Tagging both men wasn't feasible, and Farouk's true identity was a mystery to Jane.

"It's a wonderful space," Jane said, walking toward the balcony. She tried the door with her left hand, pretending it was stuck. "I can't seem to open it."

Tamimi exchanged a brief look with Farouk before moving to assist her, "Allow me," he said, stepping past.

With Tamimi's back turned and Farouk focused on the lock, Jane seized the opportunity.

Checking that the patch was still securely attached to her fingernail, Jane swiftly brushed the side of Tamimi's neck in what seemed like innocent gesture, affixing the patch.

"Oh my gosh, I'm so sorry," she said, pulling her hand away quickly. "There was a mosquito on your neck, and I reacted. I have a fear of them." Summoning all her acting skills, Jane added three words she would never say to Number Ten under any other circumstance. "Please forgive me."

Frank Turner, a.k.a. Faisal Tamimi, a.k.a. Ten, palmed the side of his neck, his eyes blazing with anger. She'd touched him, a clear violation in his world where physical contact between them was forbidden, and her action a blatant transgression. It was *Ikhtilat*. And yet, this man had no problem raping a U.S. Marine.

"West Nile Virus," Jane added, averting her eyes to better sell her act. "My grandmother died of it. I apologize."

Tamimi opened the door with ease, turning to Jane, who managed a stifled grin. "Guess it needed a man's touch."

Ten adjusted his shoulders. "Please do not touch me, Miss Henry."

"Again, I apologize." Jane turned away, unable to hide the joy she felt while angering him. She loved getting under his skin.

Tamimi's face twisted with displeasure before morphing into a smarmy smile. "The second bedroom is smaller but still large, considering real estate in New York City. Where are you coming from?" he asked, finally showing a genuine interest and looking directly at Jane for the first time. She turned away, hoping he wouldn't be able to place her. Jane hoped her red hair was enough for him not to question his own memories.

"Sweden," Jane said, telling the truth. "I was a student there for years, but now I'm back in the United States."

Tamimi cocked his head. "Sweden?"

"The apartment is staged, correct?" she asked, changing the subject and walking away.

"It is," he said. "But I work closely with the company, and if you're interested in any of the furniture, I will make the arrangements."

Jane turned on her heel, not wanting to be in the presence of Faisal Tamimi any longer. Now that the VitalWatch patch was firmly on his skin, she was anxious to get to her laptop and activate it. "It *is* very nice. Let me think about it."

Tamimi's nostrils flared, and Jane knew she'd pissed him off. She'd wasted his time—and worse, she'd touched him. "It won't stay on the market. If you're interested, you should make an offer today," he said. "Check with your husband."

Jane watched Tamimi as he locked the front door to the apartment, Mr. Farouk already making his way down the hall to call for the elevator.

"No husband," Jane said, with a shrug. "And there are other properties I want to consider."

"Are you working with another agent?"

"Yes," Jane said, recalling a folder in the hands of a businessman while on the 2 train to Kelly's apartment. *Ari Fleishman Real Estate Group.* "Ari Fleishman."

Tamimi grunted, his chin jutting forward in apparent disgust. He quickly opened and closed his portfolio before handing her a card. "I'll give you my card anyway. Ari's people could've shown the apartment themselves," he said, his tone curt. "Why call me?"

Jane eyed the crisp new business card that matched the one in her pocket. "When I saw your name on the listing, I figured I could get in to see it faster if I dealt with you directly."

"Fleishman has a reputation for not returning calls," Tamimi said, extending an arm for Jane to walk to the elevator.

"I'm going to take the stairs if that's okay," Jane

said with a casual smile. She'd reached her limit for masking her genuine emotions. More than anything, Jane wanted to headbutt Number Ten, take him to the floor, and put a knee on his neck. Then, just before slitting his throat, she would let him know exactly who she was—and remind him how he'd raped and murdered her best friend.

Qisas. An eye for an eye.

"Fine," Tamimi said with disdain, promptly turning his back to join his friend in the open elevator.

"I have your card," she said, holding it in one hand and the door to the stairwell in the other.

"Fine," he repeated as the elevator doors closed.

Once inside the stairwell, Jane caught her breath. Her adrenaline was surging, fueled by her vivid fantasies of how she might end him. She composed herself and hurried down the stairs, walking the five blocks to Kelly's apartment. It was time to set up shop.

DAY FOUR | 1700 HOURS

Dr. Peter Hudson breezed through the doors of Maxtronix Headquarters in Arlington, Virginia, latte in hand. The warmth of an early spring had coaxed the cherry blossoms into a premature bloom, but no one in the D.C. area was complaining. He'd spent his morning lecturing at Georgetown University, and while guest teaching was fun from time to time, it was a drain on Peter's time and energy.

He hurried through the first lab, nodding briefly to the engineers as he passed. His destination was the place where Maxtronix's secrets were kept—a lab six stories beneath the headquarters. Access required facial recognition, a retinal scan, and a human vein authentication key. It was a private place in the bowels of the thirty-billion-dollar defense contractor where, according to Dr. Hudson, "the magic happened."

Sacred few had ever stepped foot inside the top-secret labs at Maxtronix, and Silas Prince was one of them. Peter had taken an interest in the young engineer's mind—complex and primitive in ways that made him a perfect fit for Maxtronix's deadliest research projects. For that very reason, Peter gave Silas a private lab of his own, and set him free to work on whatever his heart desired.

Peter's lab, however, was still off-limits. That very private, soundproofed, and debugged location had never been breached by anyone. He worked there alone and had only invited Matt Matthews into his sacred space once—to demonstrate the Mia V, a nanodrone disguised as a mosquito and armed with tetrodotoxin—a poison twelve hundred times more lethal than cyanide. A lethal dose could fit on the head of a pin.

Now, utilizing technology taken from Jane's own lab in Stockholm, Dr. Peter Hudson had perfected something far more dangerous. What Jane had started with her VitalWatch project, Peter had pushed to lethal new heights. His version didn't merely record audio, video, and vitals—it could kill.

The key lay in the facial recognition software Peter had integrated into the patch, which aggregated data from surveillance cameras worldwide. From airports to public streets, the program scanned faces with surgical precision, measuring every feature—nose shape, eye distance—logging every detail.

With help from an inside operative in Stockholm, Peter's Maxtronix version of the nano-biotech had evolved into something terrifying. It didn't need a drone, a SEAL team, or a single bullet to kill. It could identify, track, and eliminate targets autonomously. Microscopic and undetectable by the naked eye, it was ready for deployment. Currently, only one test subject was wearing what Peter had dubbed the VWatch2—and his name was Silas Prince.

Sitting at a bank of computers, Peter pulled up the

live footage of Silas in the lab. With a few clicks, he rewound the feed, watching as Silas engaged in a heated conversation with Jane. Silas's heart rate spiked, and Peter turned up the audio just in time to catch the argument escalating. As Jane dominated the kid, Silas's vitals reached a boiling point right before he called her a whore. Peter chuckled, fully aware that Jane understood and spoke as many languages as Silas—including Farsi.

A single secure phone line ran to Peter's lab, so when it rang, he knew it was Matteo. "Hello," Peter said, answering without hesitation. "Where are you?"

"On my way back from Greenbriar, West Virginia," Matteo said, his voice heavy with fatigue.

"Did you get the Speaker of the House tucked away nicely?"

"He's in one of the secret cottages, guarded around the clock. He's not going anywhere but crazy," Matteo replied. "How did it go with his wife and daughters?"

"I've not heard as of yet. Funeral arrangements have been made, so I assume everything went according to plan."

"And our boy? What's he been up to?"

"Aside from calling Jane a whore?"

Matteo laughed. "I saw that coming from a mile away. They're too much alike to get along."

Peter's smile widened. "Very true, my love. Get home safe. I'll see you at the office?"

"Roger that. Landing soon."

"Good. We have a busy week ahead."

———

PETER SAT behind his very public desk at Maxtronix Headquarters, staring at the GPS signal on Matt Matthews' BMW. Jane had left her meeting abruptly, and Peter was forced to have the car retrieved and brought back to the Potomac house.

"Knock, knock."

Peter looked up to see Silas Prince leaning against the doorframe, laptop tucked under his arm.

"What can I do for you, Mr. Prince?" he asked with a smile.

Silas strolled into the office and sank into one of the heavy leather chairs—a seat that had witnessed countless battles—both on the field and in more subtle forms of warfare. "I spoke with Jane...*briefly*."

"I see," Peter said, watching the blip on his monitor move. The BMW had been retrieved and was making its way home.

"She's...*difficult*," Silas said, his voice tight with frustration. "Not much of a communicator."

Peter tore his attention away from the monitor, locking eyes with Silas. "No, I'm afraid she's not."

"I got her on the phone, and she's just...so—"

"What?" Peter asked, curious how Silas would frame calling Jane a whore.

"Dismissive. She talks down to me, Dr. Hudson."

Peter studied him carefully, noting the fire in the young man's eyes. "Jane respects hierarchy, Silas. You'll need to prove yourself to her."

Jane was an enigma. The more Peter had tried to help her, the more she'd pushed him away. He'd always wanted Jane to join forces with him—to do good in the world—but what he'd learned was that Jane wasn't about doing good. Jane was about doing what was right. And to her, those two things weren't always the same.

In the year Peter had known Jane, she often spoke in grand, sweeping terms about what she desired for her life. What she refused to talk about was Matt or the company. Peter had always assumed Jane was still haunted by what happened. She'd killed her own father—a man she'd hunted for years, unaware of his true identity—and watched Matt sacrifice his own life so that she might live.

Peter knew the heavy guilt Jane carried with her. While he was certain Matt Matthews had willingly given up his life for hers, Peter also saw the deep sadness that lingered within Jane. And despite Kelly Casey's efforts to make her happy, it seemed Jane's heart had yet to find a path toward peace and healing.

Peter wasn't sure how the last six years in Stockholm had treated her, but she seemed at least slightly changed. Jane was still brilliant, savvy, funny, and innovative but most certainly closed off when it came to her personal relationships. That, Peter concluded, was what made her both skeptical of love and the architect of her own unhappiness.

"I need to prove myself?" Silas asked with disdain. "To *her*?"

Peter could've explained the reasons why Jane was who she was, but instead, he simply replied, "Yes."

"You know, for someone who hunts and tracks extremists, she sure does operate like one."

"What do you mean?" Peter asked.

"Nothing is given. You have to earn everything. It's just like the Taliban. If you want to lead, you have to show courage and tenancy."

Peter's eyes narrowed. "I don't know if *leader* is the right word. Jane is more of a lone wolf."

"A lone wolf is a visionary, Dr. Hudson." Silas seemed to retreat into his own head, a somber voice replacing his usual tone. "Someone has to take the lead and step into the unknown. How else do you discover what you're capable of? How else do you know which path was divinely created for you?"

"A curious statement," Peter said, trying to read into the young man.

Silas shrugged. "Maybe I just need to get to know her better. I've packed up the slaughterbot prototype you wanted her to have. I thought I'd take it to her myself." Silas pulled a Post-it from the front pocket of his lab coat and slid it across the desk.

Peter looked at the address written in red ink and sighed, uncertain of what to do. Allowing Silas to go to New York would give him time to review the young man's findings, tests, and notes. At Maxtronix, it was routine practice to conduct regular and unannounced checks of a developer's work. Every workstation had a built-in backdoor that only Peter could access. It was a safeguard to ensure the PhDs at Maxtronix weren't selling off ideas to foreign adversaries. Peter hadn't had the chance to check Silas's work in weeks.

"I don't know, Silas," Peter said. "The two of you are a bit like gasoline and matches—and *you're* definitely the spark. I think you intentionally try to anger Jane."

"Anger her?" Silas asked, outwardly offended.

"Yes, Silas. You have a need to let everyone in the room know you're the smartest guy. That might not be the case if you're standing next to Jane. I think you sensed that from the moment you met her. Unless there's another explanation for your behavior. Do you have a crush or something and don't know how to act accordingly in her presence?"

Silas shook his head with confidence. "*That's* not it. She's, ah … *not my type*."

"What? A woman?"

"I'm *not* a homosexual if that's what you're implying, Dr. Hudson," Silas said, a tinge of anger in both his voice and face.

Peter took a beat, turning to glare at Silas with a single evil eye. "Be careful, Mr. Prince. Don't bite the hand that feeds you."

The room fell silent. Peter had struck a nerve, and he knew it.

"That's not what I meant, Dr. Hudson," Silas said, breaking the tension. "I was just making the point that I am not physically attracted to Jane. *At all*."

"Duly noted," Peter replied, his tone slightly clipped. "Then why, may I ask, should I send you to meet with her personally?" He watched Silas search for an answer. "Nothing you've done or said so far has instilled confidence in me that you have a legitimate reason to meet with Jane in person."

"Honestly?"

"Well, I'd prefer you not lie to me."

"I wanted to show her the work I've done on the Artificial Intelligence component of the facial recognition software and how it integrates with the slaughterbot."

Peter slid the Post-it back across the table.

Silas shrugged his shoulders, back to his old self. "I'd like to go tonight."

Peter looked at his watch. The train was the

fastest way, but a lethal million-dollar war bot wasn't what Amtrak meant by carry-on luggage. It was a five-hour drive to New York City, and it was already after six. "Tomorrow," Peter said. "Start in the morning. You can take one of the SUVs."

Silas nodded. "Okay. But *I* was thinking I might leave tonight. I can take my own car. I want to visit a friend on the way."

"A friend?" Peter asked.

"From school. But I'll drive my car. I don't mind."

"You can leave tonight," Peter said with reluctance. "But you'll take a company car. No arguments."

"Understood. And Thank you. I'm sorry if I offended you in any way. It wasn't my intention."

Silas stood and walked away. Just as he was about to leave, Peter spoke. "I need you to leave behind your laptop. Tech is sweeping the labs and workstations for malware and bugs. It's a routine quarterly check."

Silas turned. "My laptop?"

"Mmmhmm," Peter said casually, holding out his upturned hand. "Why not just give it to me now?"

"But how will I show Jane the slaughterbot software and protocols?"

"Good point," Peter replied, noticing the relief in Silas's posture. "It will only take an hour. Leave it with me, and stop by before you drive to the city."

Silas took a shallow breath—hesitating before handing it over.

"Thank you," Peter said, placing it on his desk. "It will be here waiting for you, even if I'm not. Check with my assistant out front."

As Silas walked out of Peter's office, he passed Matteo without so much as a *hello*. Matteo stepped aside, watching him barrel through the door. "Cosa c'è che non va in lui?" he asked, wondering what was wrong.

Peter shook his head. "He wants to get to know Jane better."

"I bet he does. Buona Fortuna, eh!" Matteo said, throwing up a hand before taking the seat Silas had just vacated. "And *why* does he want to get to know her better?"

Peter shrugged. "Why do you think? They're two peas in a pod. He's taking her one of the new bots he's been working on."

"We're sweeping his electronics before he leaves, right?"

Peter nodded.

"Good. We can see what the kid's really been up to. My guess?"

"What?" Peter asked. "Don't say porn."

"Porn."

DAY FOUR | 2000 HOURS

Jane sat on the floor of Kelly's apartment, using the coffee table as a makeshift desk. Her Mac-Book glowed faintly in front of her, the slides from her thesis still scattered across the desktop. It felt like a lifetime ago—back when her world was blissfully mundane, and Wolf brought her corndogs while she worked late into the night.

"Wolf." She whispered his name aloud. How was he? Was he checking on her apartment and watering her one pathetic plant? How many times had he tried to call her? Jane knew Wolf Larrson was the type of man who worried—maybe even enough to ask her professors if they'd heard from her.

Pushing thoughts of her newly-earned PhD aside, Jane tapped her finger to close the Keynote window, forcing herself to focus on the task at hand. She opened *The Eye*—the software she'd designed to monitor anyone wearing a VitalWatch patch. Her fingers hovered over the keyboard as she initiated the program, her eyes scanning the screen.

Jane needed to activate the tiny piece of hardware she'd planted on Tamimi's neck. She could only hope he wouldn't notice the faint prick as the probes embedded themselves subcutaneously. But there was always the risk he'd scratch the implant site. After activation, the VitalWatch probes would deliver data on every vital sign within seconds—even analyzing blood type, glucose levels, and cortisol.

Jane stared at the screen in anticipation, then groaned when she realized she hadn't connected to Kelly's Wi-Fi.

"Shit."

Pausing for a moment, Jane thought back to when she lived in the apartment with Kelly. Off the floor and searching the rooms, she found the router buried in Kelly's closet. It was new and surely encrypted, especially if it had been placed there by NYPD. More importantly, Kelly had probably changed the password.

Back at her laptop, she muttered, "Only one way to find out." Jane carefully entered the old password: J@mb0_J@n3. *Jambo Jane* was one of his nicknames for her—Kelly loved how it flowed off the tongue. She knew he'd chosen the password because the Jambo Inn was where he'd fallen in love with her.

She hit return and watched the signal connect. "Cocksuckingmotherfuckingsonofabitch."

She couldn't believe her eyes. Maybe Kelly was telling the truth when he said he'd kept me around after I was gone.

With Wi-Fi secured, *The Eye* software booted up seamlessly. Inspecting the silicon sheet where she'd lifted the patch, Jane double-checked the serial number before entering it into the program. Within moments, a window appeared with a single button: *Activate.*

Her breath hitched as she sat back on her heels. Once she engaged the hardware of the patch, there was no turning back. She'd be forced to deal with Number Ten and whoever else he was working with.

Jane told herself it was different this time. This time, she could speak with Blackwood. This time, she could turn over intel and work together with Operation Thunderstruck. Because for as much as Jane didn't know about Thunderstruck, she was confident Ten was a part of a terrorist plan.

"Fuck it," she said with confidence. Gliding her finger across the trackpad, she tapped on the blue button and watched as the avatar on her screen began to spin, indicating the patch was coming online. Jane's heart hammered against her ribs. She'd seen great success in the lab, but that was a controlled environment. This was the real world, and there were no safety nets.

When the avatar stopped, a prompt appeared: *Do you wish to see the vital signs of 30305?*

"Yes," she whispered, clicking on the confirm button.

The screen burst to life, displaying Tamimi's environment in chilling detail. She also saw his weight, BMI, blood sugar level, as well as his blood pressure and heart rate. "Dude," Jane said with a chuckle. "You're a walking heart attack. Your arteries are going to take you out before anyone like me gets a chance."

She crawled across the floor to her backpack, pulling out her old phone and slotting in the fresh SIM card she'd bought earlier. Plugging the phone into a wall outlet, Jane opened *The Eye* app and immediately received a ping from the transmitter now attached to Tamimi's neck.

Jane watched his vitals, glancing between the laptop and the phone to confirm they were synchronized in real time. Then, patting herself on the back, she turned up the volume, sat back, and listened in.

Tamimi's conversation was in Arabic, and although she was a bit rusty, Jane translated with ease. She hit the record option in the software, smiling as her brainchild operated seamlessly—without a single clinical trial.

As she watched Faisal Tamimi fumble around his apartment, Jane was so focused on him fixing his dinner that she didn't hear the front door of the apartment open and close. While Tamimi talked to himself, Jane shook her head in amazement. "Holy shit," she murmured.

"*Holy shit,*" Kelly echoed.

With a gasp, Jane turned, whipping the gun from her waistband. She was on her feet and ready to fire, then quickly lowered the weapon when she saw him.

Kelly.

He stood there with his hands raised in mock surrender, a weary smile dancing across his lips. It didn't last long. His eyes drifted to the scene unfolding on Jane's laptop, and a veil of concern covered his face as he moved closer.

"Why the hell is Faisal Tamimi on your laptop? Are you recording him?" he asked, his voice tight.

Jane smirked, tucking the gun back into her waistband. "Something like that. We need to talk."

———

JANE'S EYES tracked Kelly as he entered the living room. The suit was gone, replaced by gray sweatpants and a tank top that revealed the lean, muscular build she remembered so well. Jane couldn't help but smile when she noticed the tattoo—a simple lowercase *j* on the inside of his left bicep. It wasn't as bold or elaborate as his Saint Michael tattoo, but it held meaning. It was *her* letter, and he hadn't removed it.

As Kelly walked past her, Jane caught herself smiling, wondering if he'd worn the tank top on purpose—to quietly reassure her that she was still a part of him, even after all these years.

Sitting on the floor, Jane continued to watch the screen. Since she'd activated the patch, there had been no significant activity. Tamimi was asleep, his soft snores audible through the laptop speakers.

Kelly joined her on the floor. The show on her laptop was uneventful, and Jane knew it was only a matter of time before he began asking all the questions he'd been holding in for the past six years.

"Why did you come back?" His voice was soft, almost resigned.

Jane blinked. It wasn't the question she'd anticipated. "Why did I come *back*?"

"Yeah," he said, glancing briefly at the boring nightlife of Faisal Tamimi without comment. "*Then*, we can talk about *why* and *how* you're watching this asshole sleep."

Jane sighed, gathering her notebook, knife, and Glock as if preparing to leave. "I can go if you want me to."

Kelly's arm came down, strong and firm, stopping her. "I don't want you to leave. I want you to talk to me."

Jane paused, lowering her things, and turned to face him. If she'd forgotten how handsome Kelly Casey was, she was quickly reminded. His familiar blue eyes—the same eyes that had captivated her years ago—were locked on hers.

"Are you asking why I came back to your apartment after this morning," Jane began carefully, "or why I came back to the States?"

His gaze shifted between her eyes and her lips, his voice a soft rumble. "Yes."

"*Kelly*," Jane started, but he cut her off with a tone she knew so well—one that demanded the truth.

"I think I deserve to know, Jane. I spent years looking for you. *Years*. You left without saying good-bye. I woke up one morning, and you were just...*gone*. No note. No, see ya later. Not even a *kiss my ass*."

Jane's throat tightened. "I'm pretty sure we told each other to fuck off," she said, looking away.

Kelly reached over, gently placing his finger under her chin, guiding her gaze back to him. "But we never said goodbye."

Jane studied Kelly's face. He was older—they both were—but he was the same man she'd once loved. "No," she whispered. "We didn't."

Kelly breathed in, gently taking Jane's hand in his, tracing slow, delicate circles on the inside of her wrist. "Tell me about your life."

Her heart clenched at the vulnerability in both his touch and his question. "What do you want to know?"

His voice softened, his eyes searching hers. "Have you been ... *happy*? Did you fall in love in

Sweden? Is there someone waiting for you to come back?"

Jane hesitated, biting her lip. "Yes. No. Yes."

Kelly pulled away. "Yes, no, yes?"

Jane sighed. "Yes, I've been happy. No, I didn't fall in love in Sweden."

"But someone *is* waiting for you."

Jane shrugged and looked away, trying to deflect the sudden shift in the room's atmosphere. "It's not like you and the senator's daughter."

"How did you know about—"

Jane nodded toward a framed photo of Kelly and Christina on the end table. "Hard to miss. By the way, thanks for giving her a drawer," Jane said with a tiny laugh. "I'm wearing her bra and panties."

Kelly smirked, his eyes drifting south to her cleavage. "I'm sure you look spectacular in them."

Jane glanced around the room. "Is all this her doing?"

"What do *you* think?"

"I don't think she lives here. A woman like her needs more than a drawer and a bottle of shampoo."

"Making it all the easier to pack it up." Kelly chuckled, but his expression remained serious.

Jane looked up at him, her eyes blinking in surprise. It was then she noticed his gaze had never wavered. "What?" she asked.

Kelly furrowed his brow. "It's over. I told her I'd pack up her things and have them sent to her."

"And your *things* at her place?"

A sarcastic laugh escaped Kelly's lips. "Probably in the dumpster behind her building by now."

"Am I to believe you are the one who said goodbye?"

Kelly nodded, his expression softening. "Yeah."

Jane's voice broke slightly, but she kept her composure. "Mind if I ask why?"

"After the last few days—the MTA explosion, the attempt on Speaker Pearl's life—I realized Christina and I weren't on the same page. I wanted, or rather *needed,* something more. Call me a hopeless romantic, but I want what my parents had."

"So…she didn't want to marry you?"

Kelly shook his head. "I never asked."

"Then why were you with her for all that time?"

"It wasn't that long."

"It was long enough for her to redecorate your life."

"I was filling time and space. You know, *waiting,*" Kelly said with a shrug. "Enough about me —who's the guy you've got waiting for *you* in Stockholm? Some blond-haired, blue-eyed Swede who speaks five languages?"

Jane threw her head back in laughter. "He *is* blond. That much is true."

"Do you love him?"

"Did you love *her*?"

Kelly's answer was immediate. "No."

Jane hesitated.

"Shit," Kelly mumbled.

She reached out, her fingers brushing his forearm and felt him flinch beneath her touch. "I didn't love him. He was kind to me, and he knew when to leave me alone."

Kelly's eyes darkened. "And I *didn't* know when to leave you alone."

Jane stood up and headed for the kitchen, needing space, but Kelly was behind her every step of the way. When she closed the refrigerator door, he was there, pinning her against it.

Jane gripped a cold bottle of water in her right hand, her pulse quickening as she met Kelly's intense gaze.

"Tell me what you want, Jane." His voice was low and magnetic, drawing her closer without a single touch. "No games, no lies. This is me. I know you—every inch, every thought—better than anyone."

Jane not only listened to his words; she heard them. She felt the heat of his body against hers, his intensity pulling her in. And for a brief moment, she allowed herself to fall back into the memory of what they once shared.

Kelly Casey *did* know her better than anyone. Yet, despite all of his keen perception and deep understanding, he could never fully understand Jane's love for Matt. When Jane, uncharacteristically, felt the need to talk about that day, Kelly would shut down—his jealousy overshadowing his desire to help her process the unfamiliar emotions she was struggling with. Jane wanted to work through those feelings with the man she loved—Kelly. But in the end, his envy made her feel as if he'd emotionally checked out when she needed him the most.

For a woman who'd never allowed herself to be vulnerable, Kelly's unwillingness to listen without judgment felt like a betrayal of her trust. It was what pushed Jane over the edge, causing her to pack up and leave.

Jane cupped his clean-shaven face in her hand, her voice barely a whisper. "You *do* know me. And I know *you*. And I know you couldn't find your way past my feelings for Matt." Jane took a beat. "You were jealous of a dead man."

Kelly's eyes softened, and he dropped his head into Jane's hand, kissing the inside of her palm as she held it steadily against his face. "I was. But…" He hesitated, then placed his hands on Jane's hips, pulling her in. "I've worked on myself—a lot—while you've been away. Not to be better for anyone else, but to be better for me. I've learned there's room in our relationship to respect and honor all that Matt meant to you because it doesn't diminish what *we* have together."

Jane's expression softened at his words.

"What you shared with Matt is something only the two of you can understand, and I never want you to forget that part of your life. I just felt like I was your second choice—like I was a backup, even though you never treated me that way. It was my own insecurities that fueled those emotions."

"Kelly—"

He gently placed a single finger over Jane's lips, signaling that he wasn't finished. "What you had with Matt was special. Just as what we have—*had*—was special. The one thing I know with every part of me, is that I love you, Jane. I feel it in every breath, in every thought. It's been true since the moment I met you, and it still is, no matter how much time passes. Last night, I thought I was dreaming—I dream about you all the time. I call out to you in my sleep—a fact that hasn't exactly gone over well at times. But when I saw you—"

"Brandishing my weapon and ready to shoot you in the head?"

Kelly chuckled. "I admit, my dreams of you are more…"

"Civil?" Jane asked, her eyes wide with animated curiosity.

"Sexual," he murmured."

Jane bit down on her bottom lip, fighting back a smile.

Kelly exhaled, wrapping his arms around Jane and pulling her within a breath of his open mouth. "All I want to say is, I'm sorry for how I was, but I'm not sorry for how I feel. And I'm *definitely* not sorry for wanting, right now, to carry you into the bedroom and make love to you like it's our first time."

Jane glanced over Kelly's shoulder, catching a good look at her laptop screen. Kelly did the same. Ten was fast asleep, his muffled snores audible on the speakers.

"We're gonna come back to that," Kelly said. "But if he can sleep, then why can't we—"

Before he could finish, Jane gripped the back of his neck, pulling him down to her mouth for a deep, lingering kiss. When she finally allowed him to surface for air, Kelly scooped her into his arms and carried her to the bedroom they once shared.

———

JANE LAY breathless on her side in bed, the laptop open on the nightstand beside her. Kelly spooned her from behind, wrapping himself around her like a python and squeezing her just as tightly. Jane watched Ten, now asleep in his bed instead of the recliner where she'd last seen him.

Kelly's hands continued to roam up and down her

naked, spent body while she listened to his satisfied sighs in sync with Tamimi's snores. The sex had been everything she remembered—maybe more. Jane realized why she'd only slept with Wolf occasionally. Compared to Kelly, Wolf was a lot of work for a small reward. Kelly was just the opposite.

For a woman who commanded everything around her, the bed was the one place Jane allowed herself to be possessed—and only Kelly.

"I'd like to say I'd forgotten how amazing you are—how amazing *we* are together," Kelly murmured in her ear. "But I was tortured by it every day. This feels like a dream."

Jane stared at the screen, her mind racing even as her body began to relax. "In some ways, I wish it was," she whispered.

Kelly lifted his head, brushing Jane's red hair from her shoulder, creating a path to her neck for a long, soft kiss. "Don't say that."

"You know what I mean."

"Now that I've got you in my clutches," Kelly teased, "tell me everything you know about Tamimi. And don't skip the part where you plan to take him out."

Jane rolled into Kelly, nestling her head into his shoulder nook. He wrapped his arm around her, pulling her closer. "I have a better idea," she whispered. "Why don't you tell me what *you* know about Tamimi."

Kelly shifted, propping himself up on his elbow. "Intel from Homeland Security and FBI pegs him as a high-ranking thug inside an Islamic extremist group —a splinter of a Taliban cell. He's been in the United States for five years."

Jane's head snapped up. "Five years? And no one's moved on him?"

"It's hard to bust someone for selling real estate, Jane. He's kept his head down."

"How the hell did he get here?"

"Who knows? Private jet, bribed border guards, then slipped in through Mexico to join up with his brothers-in-arms?"

"Liwa Al-Intiqam," Jane said.

"What?"

"Not what. *Who.* Liwa Al-Intiqam. The Brigade of Vengeance. They're behind this. Ever heard of them?"

"No. But we're not going to arrest them tonight. Get some sleep," Kelly said, his voice softening. "You're exhausted, baby. We'll keep a close eye on Tamimi and see where he leads us."

"*Us?*" Jane climbed out of bed, pulling on Kelly's oversized shirt. "This isn't some DIY project for us to tackle together. I was pulled out of Stockholm for this. That tells me something—no *two* things: either the agencies here couldn't gather enough intel, or no one had the balls to act. Either way, I need to figure it out."

Kelly sighed, leaning back against the headboard. "Jane, you know as well as I do these extremists play the long game. They could hide out for years before taking action."

"Please don't lecture me on their tactics. I've been neck-deep in ISIS and the Taliban for years. They *always* have a plan. And I'm running out of time to figure out what it is."

Kelly's voice turned somber. "Believe me, if I had the answers, I would've stopped the bombing."

"Start there," Jane said, pacing while her mind raced. "The target was Maggie Thompson—a senator."

"Could've been a coincidence," Kelly said.

"There *are* no coincidences. Not with these people. She was a potential presidential candidate. Who else is running?"

"The president, Eleanor Shaw. It's too early to know who she'll face."

Jane stopped pacing. "And Maggie Thompson was a contender, yes?"

"Correct."

"Who else?" Jane pressed.

Kelly rattled off names, grabbing a pen to jot them down on a Post-it. "Amara Patel, the environmental advocate from California. Carlos Martinez, rags-to-riches governor of New Mexico. Nia Thompson, civil rights attorney from Texas. Wilbur Franklin, governor of New Hampshire."

Jane's mind spun at a rapid pace. "Who's polling the highest?"

"Franklin."

"And who's the closest in proximity to New York City?"

"Again, that would be Wilbur Franklin in New Hampshire. What are you getting at?"

Jane stopped pacing and looked at the clock at Kelly's bedside. "Are you still friends with that Secret Service chick?"

"Mary Charles? Yeah, I saw her today."

"What?" Jane asked, shock filling her voice. "*Why?*"

"Because I was forced to lie to a woman about her husband committing suicide and—"

"Yeah, yeah, yeah." Jane said, cutting him off as her mind cranked into high gear.

"Are you jealous, baby?"

"Call her. Someone needs to check on the governor of New Hampshire."

"Jane, it's four in the morning. What do you want me to say? That you have a hunch?"

"Yes! Kelly, please," she urged, her voice rising. "Make the call."

With a heavy sigh, Kelly dragged himself out of bed and disappeared into the next room. Jane could hear his muffled voice repeating her words. When he returned, his expression was grim. "Done. I hope you know what you're doing, Jane."

"Look, it had to be pretty damn bad for them to call me back—especially after the way I left. Something big is happening right under our noses, and we're too blind to see it." Jane stared at her laptop. "What are you dreaming about, you fat bastard?"

When she turned to Kelly, he pulled her back into bed, tucking her in beside him. "We've done what we can tonight. Let's get some sleep."

Jane stared at the ceiling, her mind spinning as she tried to make sense of it all. Just as she began to drift off, a thought hit her. "Kelly…how did you end up at Martin Pearl's apartment last night?"

"I followed Matteo," he said without hesitation.

"How did you know I was with Matteo?"

Kelly didn't answer.

"*Kelly*," she said, her voice impatient. "How did you know I was back in the States and staying with Peter and Matteo?"

He hesitated before answering. "The guy in the red scarf told me."

Matteo walked into Peter's office, two coffees in hand. "I've got some bad news and some worse news."

"Hit me," Peter said, still sweaty from his early morning workout at the office gym.

"The kid left yesterday without picking up his laptop."

Peter stared at Matteo, his expression blank. "What's the worse news?"

"There's nothing on the laptop—no files, nothing. Silas's company email is active, but it's purged every day. And it doesn't matter because he's not sending anything outside the office—only within our own network." Matteo's voice rose. "Peter, he's using a live USB. He's running his own system inside the company."

Peter took a sip of his coffee, setting it aside. "I wish I could say I was surprised, but unfortunately, I'm not."

"What are we going to do about it?" Matteo asked, his voice now filled with anger. "God only knows what he's got on that USB. He could be selling secrets to anyone, anywhere in the world."

Peter pursed his lips. "I doubt that."

"And to think I believed the worst thing we'd find on the kid's machine was porn. And why do you doubt it?" Matteo asked, catching up to Peter's comment. "He checked out Peter—his background check was clean as a whistle."

Peter nodded. "Silas Prince has an exemplary record at MIT. His parents both worked for NGOs in the Middle East. His mother even focused on humanitarian aid and women's rights after his father died."

"I don't care if his mom worked with Mother Teresa. He's up to something."

Peter's lips thinned as he wrinkled his nose. "Maybe he's more like Jane—you know, unable to trust people because of his background."

"I don't follow."

"I didn't disclose this when we brought him in, but his mother was murdered in a raid carried out by two Jihadists."

"Damnit, Peter," Matteo spat. "Why wasn't I briefed on any of this?"

Peter shrugged, taking a careful sip of his hot coffee. "It didn't have any effect on what he was capable of accomplishing at Maxtronix."

Matteo took a step away from the desk, sizing up the man he'd been married to for years. They didn't have secrets, but Matteo knew Peter was hiding something.

"Out with it, Peter. You're not fooling me."

Before Peter could answer, Matteo's phone rang. "Hold that thought," Matteo said, pointing at Peter as he answered.

"Caruso…when?"

Matteo hung up and turned to Peter. His face had gone pale.

"What is it?" Peter asked.

"It's happening."

DAY FIVE | 0900 HOURS

Jane stood at the kitchen counter, absentmindedly spreading butter on the warm toast sitting beside her Glock. She kept one eye on the laptop screen. Ten sipped tea before heading to the bathroom for his morning constitutional, flipping through the pages of a romance novel. "Did *not* see that coming," she muttered as she searched the fridge for preserves.

The apartment's intercom buzzed, immediately followed by the ring of Jane's phone. The sharp trill pulled her focus. While Kelly was in the shower, and Jane was forced to juggle both.

She grabbed the phone. "Yeah?"

"Jane, it's Matteo."

"Hold on. Someone's buzzing from downstairs." She glanced at the monitor connected to the intercom. Standing outside the building was Silas Prince, a box under his arm and an overly eager expression on his face—far too chipper for this early in the morning.

"Matteo? What the hell is Silas doing at Kelly's place?" she asked, irritation spiking her tone.

"He's delivering a bot. Peter gave him the green light."

"Perfect timing." Jane's voice dripped with sarcasm. "Alright, I'll deal with him. Thanks." She hung up before Matteo could respond, not in the mood for further explanations.

Jane pressed the intercom button, her voice clear and direct. "Silas, what are you doing here?"

"Hi Jane! I brought you a little something from the office," he said, holding up a box for the camera.

"I thought I told you I'd get it when I came back to Max HQ."

Silas's face was plastered with an annoying grin. "I didn't know when that would be, so I figured I'd hand-deliver it."

Jane rolled her eyes and buzzed him into the building. She rushed to pull on her jeans and the same red sweater from the day before. Then using her fingers, she managed a ponytail before Silas made his way from the elevator.

Just as Jane was about to open the door, she heard Ten grunt. When she turned the laptop to face her, she could see a suitcase in his hand. Jane immediately moved her computer into the bedroom, shutting the door behind her. "Shit."

A series of knocks followed, and Jane's patience wore thin. "I'm coming, dammit. Hold on."

She yanked open the door to find Silas standing there, wide-eyed and grinning. "Good morning!"

"Do you know what time it is, Silas?"

"Uh, yeah," he said, glancing at his watch. "It's just after nine. Anyway, this is the bot Dr. Hudson wanted you to have." Without waiting for an invitation, he brushed past her and strolled into the apartment.

Jane clenched her jaw. "Sure," she said under her breath. "Come on in."

Before she could regain control of the situation, Silas was on the couch, opening the box like a kid on Christmas morning.

"What are you doing?" Jane asked. "Are you seriously unboxing it right *now*?"

Silas barely looked up, his hands deftly working. "Don't you want to see how it operates?" he asked, his eyes filled with the kind of manic excitement that always set Jane's nerves on edge and her mind on high alert.

Why was Silas really at the apartment? If Jane knew anything, it was that unannounced visitors usually had ulterior motives. Why else rely on the element of surprise?

The bot was about the size of a tissue box. Jane picked it up, grumbling with annoyance.

"This is a state-of-the-art Maxtronix slaughterbot," Silas declared, snatching from her hands.

"I gathered that much."

"It's an unmanned, remotely controlled, AI-powered weapon," he continued, puffing with pride. "It can track and deliver a kill shot without human supervision, solely based on facial recognition."

Jane took a beat, studying the smug gleam in Silas's eyes. "And what exactly did *you* contribute to this...*bot*? She asked.

"I designed the artificial intelligence component," he said, stepping closer as though it impressed her. "But the real genius is in the killing mechanism. A lethal injection of X-22, delivered by a toxin-tipped dart thinner than a human hair and a quarter of an inch long. It's virtually undetectable and leaves no trace in the victim's body."

Despite herself, Jane leaned in, intrigued. "And it's completely unmanned?"

Silas nodded eagerly. "Once it receives the target's information and confirms the facial match, it's programmed with coordinates and set free to kill."

Jane took a slow, measured breath. "Can you demo it without murdering anyone?"

"I thought you'd never ask," Silas said, pulling out his phone and snapping a quick photo of Jane's face.

Jane's temper snapped with it. She gripped Silas's wrist hard. "Hand over your phone. *Now*. I'm not fucking around."

Silas yanked his arm free, defiance bubbling up like a spoiled child denied his toy. "Just a second. I want to show you how it works."

Without hesitation, Jane wrestled Silas to the ground, pressing a knee into his neck as she ripped the phone from his grip. She deleted the photo and yanked out the SIM card. Standing, she tossed the phone back to him like discarded trash. Silas lay on the floor, panting and sputtering. Jane decided he was more brat than genius, and Peter needed to keep him on a shorter leash.

Silas sneered, scrambling to gather his phone. "Too late," he said, rubbing his neck. "I already uploaded the photo to the bot's mainframe, giving it the coordinates for this apartment building."

"What?" Jane shrieked.

Silas's grin widened as he tapped his finger on the

phone's screen. "She'll find you on her own and...well..."

The bot whirred to life, lifting silently off the couch. Jane seethed with fury. "You little shit—"

"The motors have zero decibel noise," Silas said, ignoring Jane, "so death can come like a thief in the night."

"Call it off," Jane hissed through her clenched teeth.

Silas shrugged with a smug grin. "I can't. Once she's armed, there's no turning back. Think of it like a nuclear missile."

"Call it off, *now,*" Jane said, her anger boiling over as the bot tracked her movements around the room.

Silas's eyes glinted with malicious delight. "The only thing that can stop her is another slaughterbot."

The bot hovered silently in midair, lining up with Jane's face. Whatever patience Jane had left was long gone. "I'm done with your games, Silas," she said, grabbing her gun from the kitchen counter and pointing it squarely at his face. "Stand this thing down, or I will shoot you in the head." Jane took a step forward. "And then I'll shoot your bot."

Before Silas could answer or Jane could pull the trigger, Kelly burst out of the bathroom, grabbing the bot out of the air with his massive hand and slamming it to the floor with such force that it shattered like cheap glass.

"What the fuck did you do?" Silas shrieked, dropping to his knees in front of the bot.

Kelly towered over Silas, rage burning behind his eyes. "I don't know who you are or what the hell you're doing here," he said, his voice low and lethal, "but if she tells you to stand down, you stand the fuck down."

Silas trembled but shouted back. "You must be Captain Kelly Casey of the NYPD! You stupid motherfucker."

Jane watched Kelly's jaw clench, his fists balling up. Without hesitating, she stepped in, keeping her gun trained on Silas. "Enough!" she snapped, shoving Kelly back, his fury still rippling off of him in waves.

Kelly's glare shifted from Silas to Jane, his rock-hard chest softening under her palm. He stepped back, but Silas stood his ground, fixing his eyes—full of pure hatred—on Kelly.

With lightning speed, Jane spun around, shoving the barrel of her gun into Silas's ribs. "Don't be a dick, Silas. I'll throw you out the window and tell everyone you jumped." It wasn't a joke. She'd done it before.

Silas finally shifted his petulant glare to Jane, backing away from her gun. "He broke my bot."

"Who *is* this asshole?" Kelly asked, still pacing with fists clenched. Unlike Kelly, whose anger was emotional, Jane remained calm. She had ice running through her veins.

"Kelly Casey," Jane said, not lowering her gun. "Meet Silas Prince from Maxtronix research and development. Silas, this is—"

"Fuck the introductions, "Kelly said, cutting her off. "What was that?"

"A demo," Silas murmured.

"I should slap cuffs on you, you little prick. Maybe a few days at Rikers with some murderers and rapists will teach you some damn manners."

"Enough, Kelly," Jane said, with calm reserve. "I'll handle this."

Kelly's eyes burned into Silas, his muscles flexing with barely contained rage. "I know you'll handle it," he mumbled, stalking off toward the bedroom.

Silas straightened, but his voice wavered, barely masking his fear beneath a thin layer of bravado. "For the record, I'm not afraid of him."

Kelly turned, a cold sneer crossing his face. "I'm not the one you should be afraid of. Jane will gut you before breakfast and still have time for coffee."

Kelly slammed the bedroom door, leaving Silas to face Jane, her gun still in hand.

"It was a demo!" Silas shouted. "It wasn't armed. I was demonstrating the accuracy of the facial recognition."

"Now it's a pile of junk," she said, gesturing with her head to the heap on the floor.

"I'm not taking the blame for this."

Jane stepped forward, her voice dropping to a deadly whisper. "Silas, get the hell out of here."

"Hayawan," Silas mumbled under his breath, calling her an *animal* in Arabic.

Jane's patience had hit its limit. She grabbed his wrist, twisted his arm behind his back, and slammed his face into the wall with enough force to knock a photo of Kelly and his ex to the floor. "Not smart, kid," she hissed, pressing the gun into his kidney so hard he winced. "Your mouth is going to get you killed."

"What would you know about it?" he said, struggling in her grip.

"I know enough." She shoved him toward the door. "Now get out."

Silas craned his neck to the bot on the floor as Jane forced him out of the apartment. "I need to take it with me."

"It *stays*."

With a final shove, Jane slammed the door in Silas's face, leaving him pointing helplessly at the bot lying on the floor like roadkill.

Taking a deep breath, Jane walked into the bedroom to find Kelly on the phone while Ten sat in a room full of men on her laptop screen. She turned up the volume to listen in. As Kelly continued his conversation, Jane left the room, only to be called back. "Jane. *Wait*."

She pointed to her laptop and hurried to the living room to better hear the conversation. Listening intently, as the men spoke in Farsi, Jane caught fragments—someone was dead—they were victorious—the plan was moving forward. "Say a name, dammit," Jane whispered.

"Wilbur Franklin." Ten said it loud and clear.

Jane let out an exasperated sigh as Kelly sat down beside her. "Wilbur Franklin," Jane repeated.

Kelly's face tightened—his eyes dark with defeat. "He died last night. In his sleep."

DAY FIVE | 1000 HOURS

J ane sat at Kelly's kitchen table while he paced behind her, talking through every possible scenario surrounding the mysterious death of the New Hampshire governor. His voice was steady, but Jane could hear the tension beneath it.

"What do you think?" Kelly finally asked, finally stopping in his tracks.

"I need to *think*, Kelly," Jane whispered, resting her head in her palm. "I need to work it out alone. I think better when I think alone."

Kelly let out a protracted sigh. "I need to get into the office. There's still a mountain of paperwork on the MTA bombing. As soon as we get positive IDs on the suicide bombers, I'll pass it on to you."

Jane waved him off, barely looking up from her screen. Kelly fished his keys out of the blue bowl by the door. "I'll call you when I hear from Charlie. She'll have more details on Governor Franklin's death, okay?" When Jane didn't respond, Kelly's voice rose. "*Okay?*"

"I hear you, Kelly," she said, her eyes glued to the screen. "We'll catch up later."

Kelly left, and Jane turned her full attention to Ten, watching him go about his day and listening to every word. His routine seemed mundane—calls about properties, a request to refill his blood pressure medication, which ironically caused his blood pressure to spike. But it wasn't until he arrived at his office that Jane found what she was looking for. She zoomed in on his desk calendar, where the last Saturday in April was circled.

Jane's fingers flew across the keyboard, searching for the date in relation to both Washington, D.C., and New York City. When the result popped up, Jane's heart sank. "You've got to be kidding me."

The White House Correspondents' Dinner—a black-tie event filled with high-ranking politicians, power players, Hollywood elites, comedians, and nearly every notable journalist. The party—telecast live on C-SPAN and emceed by a comedian of note—was scheduled to have in excess of 2,500 attendees.

Jane quickly gathered the few belongings she'd brought with her to Kelly's apartment, locking and loading her gun. She needed to move. Now.

As she took one last look around the apartment, her eyes landed on the shattered Maxtronix bot. Scooping up the broken pieces, she stuffed them into the box and tucked it under her arm. When Jane left, she didn't return Kelly's key back in its hiding place —a silent message that she wasn't coming back.

It wasn't that Jane didn't care for him, but Kelly was a cop, bound by the rules. Jane made her own. He and his side-chick Charlie would only complicate her plan if she let them. Besides, the Secret Service was notorious for leaking information.

Jane knew what needed to be done, and she preferred to go it alone. If Jane pulled it off, perhaps Blackwood would let her off the hook. Maybe Peter Hudson would even give her a job.

As the elevator doors opened, Jane remembered Ten and his suitcase. Checking his location on her phone, her pulse quickened. He was on the move—and heading toward Penn Station.

Without hesitation, Jane downloaded the Amtrak app and booked a ticket out of the city to Union Station, Washington, D.C. If Ten was getting on a train, so was she.

———

KELLY CASEY PUSHED OPEN the door to his office, only to stop dead in his tracks. Sitting behind his desk was Senator Arthur Templeton.

Kelly's jaw tightened as he stepped into the room, his emotions a storm beneath the surface of his calm demeanor. "Senator Templeton," Kelly said, his voice breathy with unease. "What are you doing here?"

Templeton leaned back in Kelly's chair; his smug expression told Kelly he was pissed. "I came to bring you something," he said, nodding toward a small box sitting on the conference table. "I happened to be at Christina's apartment last night while she was packing up your things. Anyway," he said, forcefully clearing his throat. "She says it's all there."

Kelly's breath caught in his throat. "I, uh, haven't had time to gather her stuff. I've been a bit pre-occupied."

Templeton stood, crossing the room with slow, deliberate steps. "Look, son, I don't usually get in-volved in the love life of my only daughter, but I'm here to tell you something. If you value your career with the NYPD, you'll pick up that phone, give her a call, and beg for her forgiveness."

Kelly blenched. "I beg your pardon, sir. Are you threatening me?"

Arthur Templeton wasn't a big man—five foot nine inches at the most—but what he lacked in size, he made up for with sheer intimidation. You don't become the senator from New York without knowing how to shake down a few important people—and he'd certainly done it.

As Templeton crossed the room, Kelly could hear the man's labored wheeze with each step—no doubt the product of too many cigars. Still, Kelly stood his ground. He'd done nothing wrong, and he refused to be intimidated.

"You don't rise to power without learning how to make people bend," Templeton said with a dangerous smile. "You can drop the tough-guy act with me, Casey. I'm on to you. I know all about your little shit show from years ago—that's right, I did some digging. It's impressive what the CIA will share when you hold the purse strings. Your hands are dirtier than a subway rat. So, here's what's going to happen. You're going to call Christina and beg for her forgiveness, and then the two of you are going to spend the next few days somewhere warm and tropical. Quality time, just the two of you."

"Excuse me?" Kelly was stunned, to say the least, but he didn't flinch.

Templeton's smile twisted into something darker. "I've got friends in high places, Casey. I know all about your ex—the one with the body count. The one who killed my friend Chris Matthews and left you to clean up the mess. You'll do exactly as I say, or I'll sic my dogs on your woman. And trust me, they won't be kind when they take her out."

Templeton leaned in, tapping a finger with force into the center of Kelly's chest. "People like me don't play by the rules to get what we want, Casey. So don't ever question me again. I'm fourth in line for the presidency, and you—you're just another chess piece on the board, you stupid fucking Mick."

With that, Arthur Templeton turned and walked out, leaving Kelly standing alone, fists at his side.

As soon as the senator was gone, Kelly pulled out his phone and called Jane. There was no answer.

DAY FIVE | 1430 HOURS

Jane followed Ten onboard the 11:02 a.m. train bound for Washington, D.C. For the next three and a half hours, she sat quietly in business class, her eyes fixed on Ten and his group— the so-called Brigade of Vengeance. They mingled among the other passengers, their conversations a series of hushed whispers. Jane noticed their smiles as they glanced at newspaper headlines recounting the death of New Hampshire's governor, and the funeral of the Speaker of the House. These men were relishing in the chaos they were creating.

Jane discreetly snapped photos of each man, trying to place them on *The List.* Along with Ten, Jane recognized the faces of Hassan Najjar—also known as Twenty-Two, and Omar Al-Yazidi—Nine. The others were a mystery—young, and most likely recent recruits brought in while Jane had been out of the loop. Before, she'd always known who she was dealing with. She didn't like being the dark.

Shifting in her seat, she pulled up the Correspondents' Dinner website on her phone. She didn't need to read the details to know the stakes. There was no way she could get an invitation without making a call—and that was a call she didn't want to make. Reaching out to Blackwood was nearly impossible, and involving Kelly or Peter would only slow her down. Jane was going to handle the mission old-school and under the radar. She could apologize later. For now, she was going rogue.

When the train arrived at Union Station, she hung back, observing as the men exited separately, each using a different door. If facial recognition picked them up, they would appear as unconnected individuals—scattered. Jane's heart raced at the thought of the destruction they were planning. They only needed forty-eight hours to execute. And that's precisely how long she had to stop them.

Her eyes tracked Ten's every move—all the way to the Hilton on Connecticut Avenue—the very hotel hosting the Correspondents' Dinner.

"The balls on this guy," Jane muttered, watching him through the revolving door as he checked in.

Across the street, Jane found a much more modest hotel—eighty-five dollars a night for a private room—no questions asked. It was the kind of place she used to frequent, where you could pay in cash, and no one wanted to know your name. She checked in and got to work, opening her laptop as soon as she could get a Wi-Fi connection. She needed a better look at Ten's plans.

Jane was impressed by the incredible focus of the camera and the clarity of the audio from the Vital-Patch. Ten had worn it longer than any test subject in the lab, and it was still holding up—although Ten had yet to bathe or shower. Over his shoulder, she watched as he laid out the operation. Five suicide bombers, disguised as waitstaff, would be strategically positioned to target critical areas at the dinner—the dais and head table being prime targets. Their plan was to unleash blood and carnage live on national television. They would cry out in unison before detonating their bombs, ensuring maximum devastation.

Jane's stomach turned as she listened to them speak of martyrdom and heavenly rewards for their heinous acts. It was the same twisted rhetoric she'd encountered time and time again—Jihadist organizations using Quranic scripture to recruit and employ suicide bombers, usually preying on those burdened by their guilt from past sins. To them, martyrdom—*istishadi*— was the only path to paradise, no matter the crime or sin committed. This wasn't just about their hatred for the Western world; they believed this act was their ticket to the *Gardens beneath which rivers flow.*

These men lived in the shadows, indulging in the very vices they claimed to despise—drugs, alcohol, women—only to believe they could cleanse their souls with bloodshed. If they were going to sin, they did it big, saving their final act for martyrdom.

Jane's plan was simple: she needed entry into the dinner, and fast. Her best bet was to find a woman on the guest list—someone who wouldn't be missed. Someone whose dress and identity she could slip into.

———

MATTEO PACED in front of Peter's desk, the tension in

his posture and movements palpable. "Just tell me what to do, and I'll handle it," he said.

Peter leaned back, exuding calm. "First, you need to settle down. There's no need to panic."

"Panic?" Matteo's voice rose, his hand slamming papers onto the desk. "Peter, Silas Prince is not who he says he is. Silas Prince *was* a real kid at MIT. But the Maxtronix facial recognition program we're testing on their students is telling me that *our* Silas is a fake.

"I hear you, Matteo," Peter replied, still calm. "I'm keeping a close eye on him."

Matteo stopped pacing and locked eyes with Peter. "What if it's him? We know he's in the States. What if he's disguised himself as an MIT student? What if it's plastic surgery—something so meticulous that only *our* facial recognition software caught the discrepancies."

Peter shrugged. "Why are you so worked up about this?"

"I can't fathom why you're so nonchalant about it all. Unless…"

Peter calmly signed a document, slowly closing a folder as if it was business as usual.

"You knew." Matteo's voice dropped, as the realization dawned. "You knew all along."

The room fell into a tense silence. The two men stared at each other, their unspoken words hanging in the air.

"Out with it, Peter," Matteo demanded.

Peter's smile was faint but knowing. "Of course, it's him."

Matteo's heart pounded in his chest. "We've been harboring a terrorist? In our home?"

Peter leaned forward. "Look, Matteo, whether you know it or not, Sun Tzu was right. The best way to win a war is to outsmart your enemy before the battle begins."

"Keep your friends close and your enemies closer."

Peter nodded. "People could learn a lot from Michael Corleone."

"Where is *our* Silas now?"

"You mean after Jane nearly killed him, and her boyfriend destroyed the slaughterbot programmed to assassinate her?"

Matteo blinked, stunned. "You let that happen?"

"Of course I did. I wanted him to think he was the best. The smartest. But he was never going to get past Jane. And if by some stretch of the imagination he did, I've been watching him—every move, every step. I can disable anything he has with a Maxtronix motherboard from my phone."

Matteo sank into a chair, finally understanding. "You've been one step ahead the whole time.

"It's called strategy, my love. The art of war."

"And Jane?"

Peter leaned back in this chair. "Jane is Jane. She'll do what she does best. We just have to stay out of her way. She'll come around. Maybe. Eventually."

Matteo let out a breath, a small laugh escaping his mouth. "I don't know why I ever underestimated you, amore mio."

Peter's eyes gleamed. "Underestimating *anyone* is the most dangerous form of arrogance. And the worst mistake you can make."

DAY FIVE | 1800 HOURS

A light knock rang out at Kelly's office door. He knew it was her. He took a deep breath and said, "It's open."

Christina Templeton walked in wearing a sleek black dress that hugged her body, and sky-high stilettos showing off her tightly toned and sculpted legs, courtesy of her three-day-a-week Pilates classes.

"Wow," Kelly said. "You gotta date or something?"

She tossed her hair to one side and smiled playfully. "Daddy said you wanted to see me."

Kelly's lips tightened into a thin line, and he gave her a single heavy nod. "Yeah. About that."

She walked toward him in measured strides, her gaze burning a hole in him. Kelly knew that look—it meant one thing, and one thing only.

Pushing him back into his chair, Christina straddled him, slipping the tight dress up and over her hips to reveal black garters and stockings. Then placing her forehead against his, she ran her open palm down the front of his pants.

"Hey," he said, as she kissed her way down his

neck, then licked her way up to his mouth. "We shouldn't do this. I'm at work."

Christina dismounted Kelly's body without uttering a word. Sliding her dress back down over her hips, she walked to the door, turning the deadbolt on its side with a loud *click*.

———

JANE WALKED through the lobby of the Hilton Hotel, staying close to the front desk. She waited until a woman about her size and height arrived with a bellhop and a luggage cart, which included an elaborate dress bag emblazoned with the word *Gucci*.

"Checking in," she said, a faint southern accent dancing through her words. "Name's Ava Arable."

"Yes, Miss Arable," said the smiling guest relations clerk. "May I see a form of identification? We'll also need a credit card to keep on file while you're with us for the next two nights."

To Jane, Ava Arable didn't look like she was anyone too important—but just important enough to have scored herself an invitation to the dinner. Jane felt a twinge of guilt for what she was about to do. While Jane was about to ruin Ava's night at the White House Correspondents' Dinner, she knew it would save the lives of hundreds. Ava didn't know it yet, but she was about to perform her patriotic duty.

Jane listened carefully for Ava's room number: six, zero, one. She sidled up beside her, picking up a brochure, nonchalantly placing her foot next to Ava's. Not only could Jane most likely wear her dress, but her shoes would fit as well.

Turning on a dime, she left the hotel and headed

to a nearby drugstore, where she purchased nitrile exam gloves, makeup, tweezers, a manicure kit, a small hairbrush to fit into an evening bag, a pair of bifocal glasses, a cheap sparkly bracelet, and powdered laxatives.

When she got back to her own room, Jane checked on Ten's activity. She watched as he read through documents—all written in Arabic. From everything she could see over his shoulder, their plan was a *go*.

Jane unpacked her purchases and sat back, assessing what she had to work with. In addition to her drugstore haul, she had two guns, two knives, about five grand in cash, two phones, one broken drone, and Matt Matthews' scarf. It wasn't much, but she'd made do with less.

Curious, she opened the drone, carefully dismantling its internal components bit by bit, using the drugstore tweezers. She had countless questions for Peter about the slaughterbot's inner workings and its facial recognition software. Jane believed if the tiny microchip could handle one more component, it would be a perfect addition to VitalWatch.

When she reached the bot's ammunition compartment, she took extra care opening it. Even though Silas had assured her the drone wasn't armed, Jane didn't trust anything that came out of his mouth— especially after his reckless demo of the bot.

Under the glow of the hotel lamp, Jane pried open the housing compartment and was pleasantly surprised. Inside she found what looked like rows of silky hair-thin strands. If Silas was telling the truth, these were micro-darts tipped with X-22.

"Bingo, motherfuckers."

Kelly Casey sat in Christina's posh apartment, his third glass of Irish whiskey in his hand. After leaving his office, he'd brought her home. She was under the distinct impression—thanks to her father—that the two of them were flying to Barbados for a quick getaway.

"*Arthur Templeton.*" Kelly spat the name out between his clenched teeth before downing the rest of his whiskey and turning on the TV. "I'm fourth in line for the presidency. Whatever, dickweed," he whispered, mocking the man who'd threatened his career just hours ago.

As Kelly said the words out loud, he remembered the Post-it note in his pocket. President, VP, Speaker of the House. If they all somehow died at the same time, who takes over? A quick Google search confirmed what Kelly already knew: Arthur Templeton was elected president pro tempore as the senior member of the majority party months ago. This meant if a catastrophic attack happened and the top three leaders were dead, Arthur Templeton would become acting president of the United States.

Kelly stepped outside onto the terrace of Christina's apartment to try calling Jane one more time. When she didn't pick up, he walked back inside, the national news now playing.

"*Kelly*," Christina said, using the remote to turn down the volume. "Why is it so loud?"

He shrugged, stuffing the Post-it and his hands into his pockets.

"I'm almost packed," she said. "Then we can go to your place."

Kelly had stopped listening to Christina by the word *packed,* instead focusing on the network news.

"Preparations are underway for tomorrow night's White House Correspondents' Dinner in Washington, D.C. Network media stars, as well celebrities, are all set to party in the nation's capital for one night. The event, always full of comedic moments, will also honor several journalists from newspapers and television. Scheduled to speak are both Vice President Dorian White and President Eleanor Shaw, who famously brought the house down last year with her speech."

"That's it," Kelly muttered, staring into the screen. "That's *it*."

"What's *it*?" Christina asked, trading looks between the TV and his stunned expression.

Kelly turned to her, all smiles and sunshine. "Sweetheart, do you have a ball gown handy?"

"What?"

"Do *I* have a surprise for *you*."

U p and planning early, Jane walked to the hotel, slipping inside the building with the multitudes reporting for work through the back entrance. Most were grumbling about the extra security, the early hour, and the fact that they'd all be working overtime for the dinner. Keeping her head down, Jane grabbed a waitstaff uniform and a badge from the back of a bathroom door.

Jane knew Ava was having breakfast delivered to her room at 7:15 a.m. She'd arranged it herself after finding Miss Arable on social media and spotting a photo of her favorite breakfast. From the few details provided, Jane knew Ava liked her eggs scrambled with cheese, her bacon crisp, and rye toast. It's exactly what Jane ordered.

Standing in the hallway off the kitchen, Jane for the order destined for room 601. When it was ready, she cut the line and took the tray before another attendant could reach it. At first there was a protest, and Jane heard, "No, bitch." But when Jane slipped him a twenty, all was forgiven.

Down a deserted hallway, Jane paused, lifted the

cloche, and sprinkled more than enough laxative powder onto the eggs to ensure Ava Arable would be sidelined from the White House Correspondents' dinner.

Jane rapped at the door. Ava answered, sleepy-faced and confused.

"What's this?"

"Good morning, Miss Arable. I have your breakfast, if you'll allow me to set it up."

"There must be some mistake," Ava said. "I didn't order breakfast."

"Miss Ava Arable?" Jane said with authority. "You're here for the Correspondents' Dinner tonight. Correct?"

"Yes. Was breakfast included in my package?"

"Eggs scrambled with cheese, crisp bacon and rye toast? Sign here," Jane said, ignoring her question. "Is there anything else I can get for you?"

"No," Ava said, now awake and smiling with surprise. "This looks great. Thank you."

Jane turned, casing the room as Ava settled in behind the table. The closet containing the dress bag and shoes was by the door. What Jane wanted, was the invitation. When she finally spotted it on the opposite side of the room, tucked under a sparkling clutch, she went back in.

"I'm sorry. Please excuse me. Let me adjust this table," Jane said, kneeling to the floor. "I don't want your breakfast ending up in your lap."

"Oh, okay," Ava said, glancing underneath the tablecloth as Jane adjusted the lock with one hand, while palming the invitation and clutch from the table with the other.

Standing, Jane quickly stuffed both into the waistband of her pants, backing out of the room.

————

JANE SAT cross-legged on top of a threadbare towel on the floor of her dive hotel. Wearing rubber gloves and bifocal glasses, she carefully removed the hair-like fibers from the drone, one by one. Studying them closely, she noticed one end was pointed, the other blunt. It was subtle, but noticeable with magnification.

Strand by strand, Jane gathered the highly poisonous fibers, bundling them into sections, and securing them using a tiny sliver of tape. When she'd crafted eight small weapons of death, she grabbed the hairbrush from the drugstore bag, placing each bundle into the bristles, making sure they were secure. When she was finished, Jane held the hairbrush up for inspection.

Tonight, when she was asked to empty the contents of her evening bag—and security *would* ask— the fibers would look like hair, and Jane's weapon would make it into the party unnoticed.

She closed the purse and placed it on a rickety table by the door, catching a glimpse of herself in the mirror. Jane smoothed her hair with her hands and sighed. "Well, this isn't going to do at all."

Jane hadn't worn her hair in a bun since she'd left the military, but with the help of some gel and bobby pins, She would be sleek and ready for Ava Arable's Gucci gown in no time.

She glanced at her laptop. She'd been tracking Ten's movements all day, but while assembling the

X-22 strands, her focus had strayed. Sitting on the bed, Jane backed up the footage to ensure she'd not missed anything important.

The men gathered: Faisal Tamimi, Omar Al-Yazidi, Hassan Najjar, and a voice Jane couldn't place. When the discussion turned to the missing Tariq Maski, Jane answered the question for Yazidi. "He's not coming boys," she said, thinking of where she'd left his body in the alleyway.

The longer the meeting went on, the more Jane learned about Liwa Al-Intiqam—the Brigade of Vengeance. An arm of Unit 633, and splinter group of the Taliban, they had a leader amongst them, and it wasn't Ten. It was *the Prince*. Jane watched carefully, hoping to spot the new face. And although she could hear him speaking in Arabic, she couldn't see him.

As Jane was about to stop the playback, something caught her eye. When Ten looked at himself in the mirror, preening his beard. Jane saw the Prince's reflection. It was only a flash, but it was him.

Silas Prince.

Jane let the footage roll and watched in disbelief as they bowed to him, calling him. He was Prince of the Instructor. Son of SDK.

Half-brother to Jane Doe.

Jane tossed the laptop onto the bed and rushed to the bathroom to vomit.

DAY SIX | 1830 HOURS

D r. Peter Hudson and Matteo Caruso stepped onto the red carpet, moving through a sea of journalists, politicians, and celebrities, all dressed to impress in their tuxedos and evening gowns. The flash of cameras, the murmur of whispered conversations, and the presence of Washington's most powerful filled the air.

"Why do you believe she's here?" Matteo asked, his fingers fidgeting with the red silk pocket square slipping from his jacket.

Peter's eyes scanned the crowd. "Because," he said confidently. "She disappeared after learning and seeing what she needed. She's here. I'd bet my life on it."

"And him?" Matteo asked, his voice edged with unease.

"Hard to say. But if I were a betting man, I'd say yes. There's no world in which Jane discovers who he is and doesn't hunt him down."

After Peter and Matteo made their way through security and into the venue, they were shoulder to shoulder with the biggest names in network news and

Washington journalism. Peter was shaking hands left and right with House members and Senators, expertly weaving through the crowd. Matteo stuck close by, still watching for any signs of her.

One face Peter did not expect to encounter along the way was Kelly Casey.

"Dr. Hudson," Kelly said, a tight smile on his face as he pulled Christina Templeton by the hand like a child. "Fancy seeing you here."

"I must say, Kelly, I *am* surprised," Peter replied with smooth elegance before turning his attention to Christina. "And Ms. Templeton it is always a pleasure. You look lovely this evening."

Christina smiled, releasing Kelly's hand to shake Peter's. "As do you, Dr. Hudson. I adore your silver pocket square."

"Why thank you, dear. It was a gift from Matteo."

"He's the silver fox," Matteo said with a wink.

Kelly's voice dropped. "A word, Doctor?"

Peter picked up on the signal and followed Kelly, moving as far away from Christina as the packed venue allowed.

"Where is she?" Kelly demanded, his voice strained with urgency. "And don't give me some coy, mysterious answer, Peter. I need to know. Something is going down tonight. I've already alerted my buddy, Agent Charlie Madewell at the Secret Service, but whatever you know, please, I'm begging you—Jane needs to know too."

"First off," Peter said, keeping his tone hushed. "You need to calm down. Your heart rate and breathing are giving you away. I haven't seen her. I feel certain she's here, but as of yet, she hasn't shown herself to me or anyone else. Unlike you, Kelly, Jane is ice cold. She's a trained machine, son. Don't get in her way."

Kelly bristled. "Get in her way? I'm trying to help her. Look Peter, I know she can handle every asshole in this place, but that doesn't change the fact that I love her, and if she needs help, I want to be there."

Peter touched Kelly on the arm, leaning into his ear. "Jane doesn't need anyone to save her. Remember that. It will help you in the long run."

Kelly clenched his fists, his frustration simmering just below the surface. He stepped closer to Peter, his voice dropping to a whisper. "They're here, Peter. Their plan is to take out President Shaw and Vice President White. They believe they've already killed Martin Pearl, and they succeeded in getting to Wilbur Franklin and Maggie Thompson. If they take out the president and the vice president tonight, do you know who comes into power?"

"Would that be president pro tempore Arthur Templeton?" Peter asked, with detached calm.

"You got it. He's working with them. I don't know how deep it goes, but he wanted Christina out of the country and nowhere near this place tonight."

Peter's lips curled into a thin smile. "And yet here you are, Captain Casey."

Kelly pulled away to look Peter in the eye with defiance. "Yeah. And I'm not fucking going anywhere, Peter."

"Now *that* I believe," Peter replied, giving a single nod. "But you'd better get ready to use that line one more time. Because here comes Senator Templeton himself."

———

Nose to nose, Kelly felt Arthur Templeton's hot breath on his face as he spoke. The senator's voice was low and venomous. "What the fuck are you doing here?"

"Hi Daddy," Christina said, chirped, breaking away from her conversation with Matteo and stepping into the tension-filled conversation. "Surprise!"

Templeton's face tightened as he turned toward her, clearly taken aback. "Christina? What are you doing here? You're supposed to be on the beach," he said, the last word dripping with frustrated anger as his glare shifted back to Kelly. "In Barbados."

"Kelly had tickets to tonight's dinner, and I had a ball gown, so here we are," she said with a smile, oblivious to the volatile standoff.

Templeton's jaw clenched, his tone darkening. "Well, you can't stay, honey."

The smile faded from Christina's face, confusion sweeping across her flawless features. "Daddy?"

"I'm serious," he growled, stepping forward and gripping her arm. "You need to leave. *Now*."

Christina yanked her arm free, a gasp escaping her lips as heads turned toward the commotion. Her voice dropped to a hushed whisper, her eyes scanning the nearby guests as she forced a smile. "Daddy, you're embarrassing me."

Templeton's eyes hardened, his face a shade darker. "I don't give a damn. You're not staying."

Kelly stepped between them, his body shielding Christina as he squared off against the short, balding senator. "What's the problem, Arthur?" Kelly's voice was deceptively calm, but his eyes were darting about the room on high alert. "It's the White House Correspondents' dinner. The who's who of Washington is in this very room. I would think you'd want to show off your beautiful daughter," Kelly said, beaming with satisfaction. "Or is there another reason why you don't want her here tonight?"

Templeton's face flushed red, his eyes narrowing into slits. "You son of a bitch," Arthur hissed, his words a mere breath from Kelly's ear.

"I'm on to you, Arthur," Kelly said, his voice low and dangerous. "And Christina's not going anywhere. So whatever you and your *dogs* have planned for tonight—you better call it off."

"Honey?" Christina whined, reaching around her father to take Kelly's hand.

Kelly pulled her close—his arm protectively around her waist, his eyes never leaving Templeton's. "Let's find our table, sweetheart. Shall we?"

As they walked away, Kelly glanced over his shoulder, locking eyes with Templeton.

The night was far from over.

DAY SIX | 1900 HOURS

Jane stood at the back of the security line, waiting to enter the Correspondents' Dinner. The Gucci dress and shoes she'd snatched from Ava Arable's closet—while Ava cried out in misery from her hotel bathroom—fit like a glove. The tight bodice gave way to a flowing skirt, which Jane was most thankful for; she wanted the freedom to throw a roundhouse kick if necessary. The only accessory she added was a pair of long white opera gloves, which conveniently concealed the thin nitrile gloves she wore underneath.

Emptying the contents of Ava's evening bag onto the table at security, Jane was careful to put the lethal hairbrush in a small plastic baggie. "Keeps the stray hairs from touching my lipstick," she said to the guard with a charming smile.

"Yes ma'am," he replied. "You're good."

Jane breezed through the metal detector and endured a thorough sweep of her body and gown with a handheld wand. Once inside, she scanned the space, clocking the exit doors leading to the kitchen and prep areas. As she cased the rooms, her path was blocked by a woman in a black gown, headset in her ear, and a clipboard in hand.

"Name please?"

"Ava. Ava Arable," Jane said.

"Wonderful," she replied, checking off Ava's name on the clipboard. "Enjoy the evening."

Jane exhaled, gripping the evening bag in her hand as she maneuvered through the crowds, excusing herself around dozens of people in order to get to the main ballroom. Her first thought: find her targets.

Her second thought was much darker. Why did she have to come from such a screwed-up family? A killer and terrorist for a father, and now an asshole and terrorist for a half-brother who was working with the Brigade of Vengeance. For all Jane knew, he was orchestrating this entire splintered group of Jihadists.

As Jane navigated through the ballroom, she spotted an obvious female Secret Service agent. She purposely bumped into her, lifting the laminated badge from the lapel of the woman's black suit. "Sorry. It's so crowded," Jane muttered as she palmed the badge and kept moving.

Now armed with the credentials she needed, Jane located the waitstaff doors leading to the service corridors. Checking her phone, she honed in on Ten's GPS signal, praying it would lead her to the other players in this deadly game.

Keeping her head low, Jane slipped out of the party and into the dim service halls circling the ballroom. Keeping her head down, she hoped the badge now attached to the waist of her gown, was enough to keep anyone from stopping her.

As she moved through the hallways, she spotted

Omar Al-Yazidi—dressed as a waiter. But something was off. He didn't seem overly burdened by a suicide vest—at least not yet. Jane allowed him to pass, then quietly turned and followed, keeping a close eye on her surroundings. The last thing she needed was a witness.

When the hall cleared, Jane rushed forward, tripping Twenty-two to the ground with a hard *thud*. Before he could react, Jane struck him, landing a precise blow to a pressure point in his neck. Her thumb was expertly angled to hit his carotid artery He was stunned, but not unconscious.

Dragging him around the corner, Jane searched for an open door, trying each handle as she passed. Finding one, she yanked Twenty-two's body inside and quickly fished out the hairbrush from her evening bag.

"Here goes nothing," Jane muttered, just as he began to stir.

He lunged for her throat, clamping down with terrifying strength. Jane gasped for air, her fingers fumbling with the hairbrush—the opera gloves were too slick to gain any control of the fibers. Twenty-two's grip tightened, cutting off her breath.

Desperation fueled her as she gripped the end of the hairbrush, tapping the top of it to his neck. Within two seconds, his body slackened, and his hold on her released as he slumped to the floor.

Panting, Jane rubbed her throat. "Dammit," she hissed "I wasn't built for this fancy shit. Give me a bathroom at a filthy gas station any day."

Slipping off the opera gloves, she tucked one into the evening bag now slung over her shoulder, carefully concealing the lethal hairbrush inside the fold.

Improvise. Adapt. Overcome.

Back in the hallway, Jane smoothed her bun and straighten her dress, checking the signal on her phone. From the point of Twenty-two's dead body to Ten was a perfect diagonal across the ballroom floor. If they were spreading themselves out, as Jane had seen in the plans, another suicide bomber was waiting at the opposite end of the hallway.

Jane's pace quickened; her eyes sharp for any sign of her next target. Weaving in and out of the waitstaff, she finally found her way to a dead end. She stopped short just as a door flung open, revealing the main dais, where the VIPs were gathered and waiting for dinner to begin. Empty seats awaited the president and first gentleman, and the vice president, and his wife.

A head waiter walked in front of her, giving her a side glance. "Are you supposed to be back here?"

Jane turned, flashing the badge on the waist of her dress.

The waiter squinted. "*And?*"

Jane looked down, realizing she'd lost the badge in the fight with Twenty-two. "Secret Service," she said with authority.

"You don't look like Secret Service."

"And tonight, that's exactly how it should be," Jane retorted, speaking into her bracelet as if it were a hidden mic.

The waiter grumbled and moved on, leaving her at the open door.

Just across the room, Jane saw Hassan Najjar— Number Nine. Standing beside him, whispering in his ear, was none other than Senator Arthur Templeton.

Jane's pulse quickened. "Oh, let's fucking go,"

she muttered, barely containing her rush of adrenaline.

Ten's plan was now clear. Four bombers in the four corners of the main room of the Correspondents' Dinner: Ten, Twenty-Two, Nine, and the unknown man would converge into the room and detonate. Of the two she hadn't spotted; one would cover the dais and the other the overflow room.

Jane bided her time, keeping an eye on the clock. There was no way Templeton was sticking around for showtime. She stood closer to eavesdrop, hearing him say, "I don't know why that stupid Mick brought her here, but I have to get her out before. Understand?"

Jane's jaw dropped. Had Kelly brought Templeton's daughter to the dinner? Jane scanned the crowd, trying to spot him. Whether intentional or not, Kelly had created the perfect distraction, buying her precious time.

As soon as Templeton walked away, Jane tapped Nine on the shoulder, motioning for him to follow her out of the banquet hall. When he curled his lip and refused, Jane grabbed him by his ear, forcing him into the hallway.

Nine threw a punch, but Jane ducked and retaliated with a vicious right hook to his solar plexus, rendering him gasping and helpless.

A waiter passed by. "Is he okay?"

"I think so," Jane replied, feigning concern. "Can you help me get him outside? I think he needs some air?"

Together, they walked Nine out of the building and into the night air.. He cursed in Arabic the whole way. "Leave him with me," Jane said.

The moment they were alone, Jane didn't hesitate. She junk-punched Nine, watching him crumple to the pavement. Reaching into her purse, she carefully pulled out a bundle of fibers armed with X-22 and stabbed him in the neck.

Hassan Najjar, aka Nine, was gone in less than three seconds.

Jane rushed back inside and realized, in order to make it to Ten, she would have to cross the crowded banquet hall virtually unseen. Snaking her way through the sea of guests, Jane hid behind a tall man as he walked in the same general direction. As she concealed herself in the crowd, she saw the fourth man of Ten's band of soldiers.

Jane followed him to the back of the room. When she had enough room, she pulled the brush from her purse, taking another bundle of X-22 fibers precariously by the end.

When a member of the hotel staff left a storage closet near the restrooms, she seized the moment, inconspicuously tapping him on the top of the hand, then bum-rushing him into the storage closet after catching it with her foot. Jane tossed him inside to die alone.

But the clock was ticking. If Ten tried to communicate with his men, he'd know something was wrong. Jane couldn't risk him detonating anything when he discovered the plan was compromised.

Walking back into the main dining room, Jane took a full breath, her adrenaline now kicking into high gear. And then she saw him. Ten. Panic filled Faisal Tamimi's face as Jane marched toward him through the crowd.

While he fumbled with his phone, Jane shoved him out the door and into the hallway. If he was going to detonate, Jane had to get him away from the others.

The confrontation drew attention. Security and attendees alike were now watching the chaos unfold.

Jane could hear gasps and plates hitting the ground inside the gala, but Number Ten was her only focus. Jane didn't want him unconscious—she wanted Ten aware of everything that was happening. She landed a brutal right hook to his face, sending him staggering. He tried to fight back, and Jane smiled.

Ten had lived in America for so long, he'd gotten fat and lazy. He was no longer proficient in hand-to hand-combat. Jane was.

With a direct right hook to the nose, Ten hit the ground, Jane grabbed him by the wrist, dragging him out the door and into an alleyway beside the hotel.

Throwing open the hotel uniform, Jane saw the bomb strapped to his chest.

Ten was dazed, but still conscience. Jane straddled him, the silk chiffon of her dress ballooning over him in an elegant puddle.

She slapped him in the face, bringing him to full consciousness. Jane then braced his wrists against the concrete, holding down his thumbs as Secret Service and others rushed on the scene.

"Stay back," Jane shouted. "He has a bomb strapped to his chest. Evacuate everyone!"

Jane eyed the detonator still in the palm of his hand and knew she had a decision to make: reach for the X-22 and end them both, or wait for Secret Service secure him, where he'd surely be—*alive*. Jane's eyes darted back and forth between Ten's face and the detonator.

"Do it," he spat, blood oozing from his mouth. "You want to kill me, bitch. But I want to kill you more."

"My name," Jane said, leaning in to whisper in Ten's face, "is Jane Doe. You murdered my friend, Lance Corporal Jennifer Drenkowski after I shot two of your men like animals."

Ten writhed beneath her. She lifted and slammed his back to the pavement once more. He stopped fighting her, but still held the detonator in his right palm with three fingers.

"Secret Service! Stand down!"

The shouting over Jane's shoulder couldn't stop her from her mission. She ignored every word, blocking out everything except the killer under her control. "On your way to hell—to *Jahannam*—I want you to remember this face. You are dying at the hands of a woman. Do you understand? There will be no virgins for you, no beautiful welcome. You are going to burn in *hellfire* and suffer with Shaitan for the rest of eternity."

Jane's chest heaved with each confident intake of breath. "Tell me you understand what I've just said to you."

"If I'm going to hell," Ten whispered, blood and spittle falling from his mouth. "I'm taking you with me."

"Get back!" Jane screamed. "Get out of here!"

Jane strained against Faisal Tamimi as he regained enough strength to fight back. She closed her eyes, pressing his thumbs to the ground as hard as she could, not seeing the shadow behind her, or hearing his voice. Jane stared at the detonator knowing this was how she went. "What's a life anyway?" she said. "We're born, we live a little while, we die."

Kelly Casey rushed to Jane, taking the remote from Ten's grip as Secret Service hurried in to secure him.

"Jane! Let go!" Kelly shouted. "Let go!"

She could see Kelly's mouth moving, but she couldn't hear his voice.

Finally, she sat back, still astride Ten, staring him in the face. The voices all around her shouted and grabbed at her, but Jane wouldn't move. Not until Ten was dead.

Looking down, Jane noticed one single fiber of X-22 clinging to the glitter on the cheap, drugstore bracelet. Pinching it between her thumb and index finger, she touched it with her bare hand, knowing the risk she was taking.

Jane then leaned in to whisper in Ten's ear. "See you in hell."

She poked the fiber into his neck, extracted it, and rolled herself off. Faisal Tamimi was dead.

Sirens, police, Secret Service, and Fire and Rescue stormed the hotel as Kelly picked Jane up off the ground, shielding her from the authorities who wanted to handcuff her as well.

In the chaos, Jane looked at Kelly and whispered, "He got away."

"No," Kelly said, shaking his head. "Secret Service apprehended the other two."

"You don't understand," Jane said. *He* got away."

DAY SEVEN | ZERO HUNDRED

J ane sat in the caterer's office surrounded by officers from every imaginable agency. She said nothing. She answered no questions, not even to state her name. Kelly stayed by her side, also silent, except to flash his badge and explain who he was. When Agent Charlie Madewell walked in, she took charge.

The hotel had been evacuated, but there was no sign of Amir bin Siad al Daleel ul Khyayraat. Jane was right. He was gone. As for Senator Arthur Templeton, he was taken into custody when several witnesses said they saw him talking to Tamimi earlier in the night.

Ed Zuckerman, Director of the United States Secret Service, eventually cleared the room—including Kelly. Jane stared at him but said nothing. When he left, closing the door behind him, she was finally alone.

Immediately on her feet to assess her possible escape routes, Jane turned when she heard the door open. Standing before her, wearing a black gown adorned with a red silk rose on the shoulder, was Wilhelmina Blackwood.

"Did you at least have a nice time?"

"No ma'am," Jane said. "I can honestly say that I didn't."

"I'm sorry to hear that. Maybe next time we can provide an exceptional experience," she said, pointing to a sign on the wall that read: *PROVIDE AN EXCEPTIONAL EXPERIENCE.*

"Did you capture him?" Jane asked, her voice barely audible.

"Who?"

Jane refused to speak his name. "*You* know who."

"No. But we did manage to get our hands on all the devices. Your friend, Agent Madewell, managed to detain the one you *didn't* kill. Maybe we can get some information out of him."

"Hmm," Jane muttered, still feeling like a failure. Without her half-brother in custody, she knew she would be haunted by the thought of him day and night.

"Jane," Blackwood said, taking her from her trance. "The president wants to thank you for your...*bravery and services* tonight. She, along with many others, owe you a great deal."

Jane looked to the ground in defeat. "I failed."

"You lived to fight another day."

Jane scoffed. "Don't you think that's a little cliché?"

"Come with me."

Jane followed Blackwood out of the office. The once-crowded hallways were now desolate. When Blackwood opened the door to the main ballroom, Jane saw nearly twenty people—all sitting at tables scattered throughout the banquet hall. They were men and women, young and old, all with one thing in common—red. Every single one of them were wearing either a red dress, a red bow tie, a red pocket square...*red.*

"Jane," Blackwood said. "This is an elite force of people who work behind the scenes around the world."

She scanned the crowd, only to find Dr. Peter Hudson and Matteo Caruso smiling at her from across the room. Closer still, was the journalist, Levi Grant.

"Jane, we'd like you to join us."

"*Join*?" Jane asked. "What about Operation Thunderstruck?"

Wilhelmina Blackwood stared Jane in the face. "*You* were Operation Thunderstruck."

"What?"

"It was you all along."

Jane looked around the room and back to Blackwood. "I don't understand. I thought the plot to murder the president and—"

"That was very real—and unexpected, if I'm being quite honest. But I'm making you an offer, Jane. A chance to join normal society as yourself... but also as one of us."

Jane looked around the room once more. Their faces were deadly serious. "Join you to do what?"

"What you do best, dear."

Jane looked for Peter once more. He cracked a smile, giving her a reassuring nod.

"Okay," Jane said. "Yes."

"Dr. Jane Ellison," Blackwood said, sweeping her arm across the room. "Welcome to Red Fox."

DAY 22 | 1300 HOURS

A cool breeze caught Jane unaware as she sat at a sidewalk café in Soho, She shivered, wrapping a red scarf around her neck before burying her nose back inside her journal. The shrink at her new employer thought it important for her to write down everything that worried her, irritated her, or that she cared about. At the moment, Kelly Casey was at the top of all three lists.

He'd broken up with Christina after her father was carted off. Of course, Templeton bailed out—it's good to have friends in high places—but he'd still have to face the music of collaborating with known terrorists, even if he did claim to know nothing about the bombs.

Ava Arable was eventually aware of what happened to her *and* her dress. Jane told her in person and apologized. For the journalist's troubles, Jane made sure she got an exclusive story about the terrorists who tried to blow up the White House Correspondents' Dinner. She thought perhaps a Pulitzer was in Ava's future.

As for Speaker of the House Martin Pearl. He

was reunited with his wife and daughters immediately. Although they were livid at first for the emotional roller coaster they were forced to endure, ultimately they were simply grateful he was, in fact, alive.

As for her half-brother—Amir bin Siad Al Daleel ul Khyayraat—he'd vanished like a ghost in the night. The real Silas Prince hadn't been found, which led Jane to believe he was dead. Amir had stolen Silas's identity to mask his own. It was a new type terrorist—one ready to leave their own life in order to step into another's for the sake of the cause.

With his access to unlimited funds, coupled with his intelligence and cunning, Amir was more dangerous than his father. But Jane was patient. And as brash as Amir had proven himself to be, Jane knew it was only a matter of time before *the prince* showed himself once more. She would be waiting.

Red Fox gave Jane the choice of where she wanted to live and what she wanted to do. After speaking with Peter, she decided to open a lab—in New York City—collaborating with Peter and Maxtronix. Without a place to live, Peter gave her the keys to the penthouse owned by the company— telling her to stay as long as she liked.

Kelly was a little upset when she moved out of his place, but they were still together. Jane needed time to figure out who she was. She wanted to learn how to love herself before she could love Kelly. They both deserved that much.

As she chewed on the end of her pen, Jane thought about where her new life might lead her. Closing her journal, she drank the last of her tea, dropping the cup back into the saucer with a crash.

Embarrassed, Jane dug into the front pocket of her jeans, looking for a few bucks to leave as a tip.

When she looked up, there he was, looming over her table like a towering oak.

Jane gasped. "Wolfgang?"

"I decided if you didn't come back to Sweden," Wolf Larrson said with a huge grin, "I'd come find you."

Jane stood to give him a hug. "I'm *shocked* to see you. How *did* you find me?"

Wolf led Jane back to her chair, sitting across from her. He opened his coat as he sat, revealing a red wool sweater.

Jane cocked her head, giving him a confused grimace. "*Wolf?*"

He took a deep breath and settled in. "I thought you should know your plant is still alive."

ABOUT THE AUTHOR

Kris Calvert is a former copywriter and PR mercenary who now writes thrillers, suspense and romance novels. She's married to an Emmy®-nominated composer, and has two grown kids. She's also responsible for one needy rescue pup. When she's not writing, she's hosting the true crime podcast Hitched 2 Homicide or baking gluten free cupcakes.

ALSO BY KRIS CALVERT

Sex, Lies & Sweet Tea – Book One
Sex, Lies & Lipstick – Book Two
Sex, Lies & Pearls – Book Three
Sex, Lies & Lace – Book Four
Sex, Lies & Bourbon - Book Five
Sex, Lies & Black Tie - Book Six
Sex, Lies & Diamonds - Book Seven
Sex, Lies & Champagne - Book Eight
Sex, Lies & Leather - Book Nine
Sex, Lies & Rock n Roll - Book Ten
Fate, Snow & Mistletoe - A Sex and Lies Holiday Novella

Jane Doe 1 Scarlett
Jane Doe 2 Alice
Jane Doe 3 Catherine
Jane Doe 4 Charlotte

Beauty

Lead Me From Temptation
Deliver Me From Evil

Be Mine – a Valentine's Day Novella
Sparks Fly – an Independence Day Novella
Roses are Wrong, Violets Taboo

Witchin' in the Kitchen - A Halloween Novella

Coming

The Fox Tales Series

Sex, Lies & Tequila

ACKNOWLEDGMENTS

Thank you to my adoring husband, **Rob** who cheered me on as I brought Jane out of retirement. And to my two children who aren't children anymore, **Luke** and **Haley** who always find time to ask about my writing about in the middle of their own busy lives. I love you all, with all my heart.